Setting the Pace

Books by Lauraine Snelling

Hawaiian Sunrise

A Secret Refuge

Daughter of Twin Oaks

Red River of the North

An Untamed Land
A New Day Rising
A Land to Call Home
The Reapers' Song
Tender Mercies
Blessing in Disguise

High Hurdles

Olympic Dreams
DJ's Challenge
Setting the Pace
Out of the Blue
Storm Clouds
Close Quarters
Moving Up
Letting Go
Raising the Bar
Class Act

Golden Filly Series

The Race
Eagle's Wings
Go for the Glory
Kentucky Dreamer
Call for Courage
Shadow Over San Mateo
Out of the Mist
Second Wind
Close Call
The Winner's Circle

Setting the Pace

LAURAINE SNELLING

BETHANY HOUSE PUBLISHERS
MINNEAPOLIS, MINNESOTA 55438

Cover illustration by Paul Casale

Published by Bethany House Publishers
A Ministry of Bethany Fellowship International
11400 Hampshire Avenue South
Minneapolis, Minnesota 55438
www.bethanyhouse.com

Printed in the United States of America by
Bethany Press International, Minneapolis, Minnesota 55438

Library of Congress Cataloging-in-Publication Data

Snelling, Lauraine.
Setting the pace / Lauraine Snelling.
p. cm. — (High hurdles ; 3)
Summary: Fourteen-year-old DJ seeks God's guidance about a riding school student's overt racism as well as about her mother's surpise announcement of plans to remarry.
ISBN 1-55661-507-8
[1. Horses—Fiction. 2. Afro-Americans—Fiction. 3. Racism—Fiction. 4. Remarriage—Fiction. 5. Christian life—Fiction.] I. Title. II. Series: Snelling, Lauraine. High hurdles ; bk. 3.
PX7.S677Sf 1996
[Fic]—dc20 95-43932
CIP
AC

To Joanie Jagoda,

who shares her horse expertise and her heart with me.

As is always the case with true friends,

my life is richer because of her,

and my books are better thanks to her input.

One day she'll be giving me riding lessons.

Yes!!!

LAURAINE SNELLING fell in love with horses by age five and never outgrew it. Her first pony, Polly, deserves a book of her own. Then there was Silver, Kit—who could easily have won the award for being the most ornery horse alive—a filly named Lisa, an asthmatic registered Quarter Horse called Rowdy, and Cimeron, who belonged to Lauraine's daughter, Marie. It is Cimeron who stars in *Tragedy on the Toutle*, Lauraine's first horse novel. All of the horses were characters, and all have joined the legions of horses who now live only in memory.

While there are no horses in Lauraine's life at the moment, she finds horses to hug in her research, and dreams, like many of you, of owning one or three again. Perhaps a Percheron, a Peruvian Paso, a . . . well, you get the picture.

Lauraine lives and writes in California with husband, Wayne, basset hound Woofer, and cockatiel Bidley. Her two sons are grown and have dogs of their own; Lauraine and Wayne often dogsit for their golden retriever granddogs. Besides writing, reading is one of her favorite pastimes.

1

"DO NOT RUSH THE JUMP!" Bridget ordered.

Straight ahead between Major's pricked ears, DJ Randall watched the brush jump draw closer with every thrust of her horse's haunches. *Now!* They lifted and flew over the jump, clean and perfect, before her mind could finish the command. Major came down on his front feet, his rear landing in perfect timing.

DJ kept her focus on the three rails of alternating height before them. Silently counting, she leaned forward, heels down and eyes straight ahead.

"Come on, boy." Her murmur was lost in the shush of hooves in the sand, the grunt of a horse giving his best effort. For a split second, they hung suspended in air.

That was the moment DJ lived for.

The clack of a back hoof on the rail sounded as loud as a cannon shot.

"Concentrate, DJ—you lost your concentration." Bridget Sommersby, trainer and owner of Briones Riding Academy, called from the center of the ring. "You got left behind."

"Fiddle."

"Come on, go around again."

DJ did as she was told, this time forcing herself to forget

the glory and count the paces.

They finished the circuit with the in and out, a jump that looked more difficult than it actually was. If horses could laugh, Major was—both he and DJ. In her case, the laugh was one of pure delight.

"Well done." DJ's mentor leaned her elbows against the aluminum rail fence. "That was as close to a perfect round as you have ever ridden, in spite of the tic." Bridget pushed her glasses further up on her nose with one finger. Her smile made DJ feel as though she'd just won the Grand Prix.

Or at least she thought it would feel that way. Since DJ had never won the Grand Prix in her fourteen years, or even been to one for that matter, she held on to the feeling for as long as she could.

She wanted to squeeze Major's neck in a hug to end all hugs, shout hallelujah, and . . . and how could she possibly act professionally, as Bridget expected? Her huge smile splintered her cheeks and her jawbone.

"Thank you." There, DJ had managed to keep the lid on her excitement.

"Wow!" Amy Yamamoto, DJ's best friend, rested her arms across her saddle horn as she and her half-Arab gelding, Josh, rode up. Josh tossed his head and nickered as if he agreed.

After shooting a raised-eyebrow look at Amy, DJ stopped Major in front of Bridget. Cheers would come later.

"We will raise the poles for your next lesson, but you must concentrate. You have a tendency to get so caught up in the thrill of the jump that you leave too much up to Major. If you were riding a horse that was not a natural jumper, you could get into difficulties."

DJ listened attentively and nodded. "Will that feeling go away with more practice?"

"I hope not." Bridget smiled up at her student. "That joy is what makes you a good rider and is why you are learning so quickly. Major feels it, too, so he gives you his best."

"I'm not sure I understand."

"The more you concentrate and focus on what you are doing, the more joy there will be for you in riding. You will understand what I mean in time." Bridget smiled again.

DJ felt the warmth of the smile encircle her and bring an answering grin to her own face. "Thanks." No other word came to mind that began to describe what she was feeling. *I'm finally jumping, I have a super-fantastic horse of my own, and if I don't get to move soon, I'm afraid I'll explode!*

"I better put Major away and get home. See you tomorrow." At Bridget's nod, DJ lightly squeezed her lower legs. Major responded immediately by heading for the gate.

"You know, horse, if I didn't know better, I'd think you understood English better'n I do." DJ patted the sweaty neck of the sixteen-hand bay. Major paused so she could swing the gate open, then walked on through, stopping again to allow the gate to be closed. "And if I didn't want to jump so badly, you'd be a sure winner in the trail class."

"You two were awesome." Amy dismounted at the same time DJ did, and together they led their horses into the red-sided pole barn. The two friends were about as opposite as could be. Amy, tiny at five feet, had flowing dark hair, almond-shaped eyes, rode Western, and thrived on hot, spicy food. At five feet seven, DJ was as long-legged as a colt, had sparkling green eyes, felt English was a far more comfortable ride, and hated peppery food. Both girls shared one major complaint—their bodies had about as many curves as a plank. Many times, DJ had sighed and noted, "Some *boys* have bigger chests than we do." Amy had to agree.

"Ames, pinch me so I know I'm not dreaming." DJ held

out her arm to her friend. "Ouch! I was only kidding."

With the reins draped over one arm, she reached up to remove her helmet and tighten the band holding her wavy blond hair in a ponytail.

Major sniffed her hair, then her jeans pocket, nosing for the treat she saved for his reward.

"Sorry, old man, you ate it earlier."

Major blew in her face, slobber and all.

"Yuck." DJ wiped the wet drops off her tanned face with the hem of her T-shirt.

The horse rubbed his nose against her chest, leaving white hairs, slobber, and sweat on the dark blue fabric.

"Now you did it. Mom will insist I change clothes before dinner."

"Well, you better hurry then. We won't be home before dark at this rate. And I have tons of homework. Besides, you don't want your mother yelling at you." Amy stripped off her Western saddle and the thick pad underneath it while she talked. Always practical, Amy did her best to keep DJ out of trouble.

"Okay, okay." DJ followed suit, setting her English saddle on one of the two-by-four bars that made up the saddle rack on the wall of the tack room. Her name was written on a three-by-five card to remind everyone that this was her private property. Most horse boarders took their gear home with them, but since DJ and Amy usually rode their bikes to the Academy, they kept their tack there.

"You *did* do your chores before you came?" Amy peered around Josh's neck when DJ didn't answer. "Didn't you?"

DJ kept quiet.

"DJ!"

"Well, I was in a hurry, and—"

"We'd really better hurry now. What time did your mom say she'd be home?"

"Seven." *And I sure hope that means eight, as usual. I*

don't know where the time goes. DJ's thoughts kept pace with the two grooming brushes she wielded with such skill. Grooming a horse had become second nature to her.

If only Gran . . . DJ clapped a lid on the thought. Gran didn't live far away, but on nights like this, her house might as well have been on the other side of the moon. She wasn't living with DJ and her mother now that she'd met and married Joe Crowder. She wouldn't be in the kitchen cooking dinner or out in her studio putting the final touches on one of her paintings for illustrated children's books.

"Earth to DJ. Come in, DJ." Amy waved her hand in front of DJ's face.

"Oh, sorry. Did you say something?"

"No, not really. I was just talking to Josh here about his homework." Amy wore a disgusted look that said she'd been expecting an answer.

"Sorry." DJ gave Major's now-dry coat a quick once over, checked the hay in the hay net, and grabbed the water bucket. "I'll be right back." While water gushed into the bucket from the spigot, she looked up toward the hills of northern California's Briones State Park. While the hills still wore the gold of fall, soon winter would bring rain and, with it, tender shoots of green grass. The oak trees were turning shades of rust and gold, the color deepened by the setting sun. Down in the hollows, the trees already looked black.

DJ shut off the water. Black trees meant black skies, and black skies meant a black mood on her mother's face and over the entire house if DJ wasn't home before dark. DJ knew she'd better put herself in gear, but she'd rather be at the Academy than anywhere else on earth.

Amy and DJ signed out on the duty roster, DJ gritting her teeth at the signature right above hers. *Tony Andrada.* He was even worse than his predecessor, James, whom she used to think was the biggest pain alive. But thanks to her grandmother's counseling, DJ and James had become friends. Unfortunately, Tony outdid James in rottenness a hundred to one.

"Have you heard from James?" As usual, Amy seemed to know what DJ was thinking.

"You blow me away."

"How?" The pair swung their legs over their bikes at the same moment, as if the move had been choreographed by a dance instructor.

"How did you know I was thinking about James?"

"I didn't." Amy shot a grin over her shoulder as they turned onto Reliez Valley Road. "So answer the question."

"So I haven't heard. You know he'd rather send e-mail than a letter, but since I don't have a computer, he has to do things the old-fashioned way. Why is it so hard to type up a letter on the computer and stick it in the mail?"

"Don't ask me, I'm not a computer nerd."

"No, you're just a horse nerd—like me." DJ panted. The second hill always made her huff.

They turned and coasted down their own street. Coming home was always easier than going to the Academy, at least as far as peddling was concerned. DJ groaned. Her mother's car sat in the driveway.

"You have company."

"Hey, you're right." DJ's groan changed to a grin. "Robert's here."

Amy turned up her drive and stopped to wave. "See ya in the morning."

"Okay." At least now, with company in the house, she wouldn't get a lecture till later. And sometimes when her mother and Robert had been swapping gooey glances, trouble disappeared altogether.

DJ dismounted and entered the front door to press the button that raised the garage door. Tonight she would make sure her bike was put away. No need to make matters worse.

"Mom, I'm home." No answer. DJ stashed her bike in the garage and reentered the house.

"DJ, is that you?"

"Who else do you suppose it would be?" DJ was careful to keep the mutter just that. "Yeah." She raised her voice to be heard outside. Obviously they were out on the deck.

"You're late."

"It's not dark yet." DJ grabbed a soda out of the refrigerator and crossed the family room, no longer Gran's studio, to the French doors leading onto the redwood deck. Robert and her mother turned to greet her.

DJ stopped as quickly as though she'd run into a glass wall. A diamond ring glinted on her mother's hand.

"Robert has asked me to marry him." Lindy looked up at the man standing just behind her, his arm around her waist.

DJ felt as if she'd been kicked in the chest by a feisty horse.

2

"HAVE YOU NOTHING TO SAY?"

DJ looked from her mother's hand to her eyes and up at Robert. "I . . . I . . ." She cleared her throat. What was she supposed to say? Hurrah and congratulations? This was her life they were planning so glibly! "I . . . ah . . . that's great." Even to her ears, the response sounded weak.

"I know this comes as a surprise to you."

Yeah, you could say that. About a hundred times over.

Robert's deep voice drew DJ's attention back from her mindless study of the ring to his face. The two lines that cut between his straight eyebrows looked deeper than they had the moment before. His gray eyes had darkened.

"I better get something to eat so I can get started on my homework." *Ask 'em when the wedding will be, bozo.* DJ headed for the kitchen. *Why would Mom take his ring if she didn't want to marry him, yo-yo brain?* DJ felt as though she had another person in her head, arguing her mother's case.

I'd have a father. Someone else to boss me around. And if Mom married Robert, those two human dynamos would be here all the time. DJ shuddered. The five-year-old twin boys, Bobby and Billy, would make St. Peter wish for a new assignment. Her smile at the thought felt stiff, like a pair of shoes left out in the rain and then dried too quickly.

She dished up food from all four take-out containers and stuck the plate in the microwave. How come two minutes of waiting for the microwave timer to beep and two minutes in the show-ring passed at such different rates of speed?

Carrying her plate up to her room, DJ stopped in the family room. "Does Gran know yet?"

Lindy shook her head. "We hoped you'd be happy for us, DJ."

"Oh, I am." DJ started up the stairs. "I am." She hurried upstairs, half worried they might chase her and shake the truth out of her. She was proud of herself for not slamming the door to her room. But then, she wasn't mad—was she?

She sat on the edge of the bed shoveling food into her mouth as if that could shut out the thought. Beef with broccoli, sweet-and-sour prawns, egg foo yong, chicken chow mein—it all tasted the same. She set the plate on her desk and cracked open her fortune cookie. *Great money is coming into your life.*

She read it again. Wouldn't that be incredible? Money she needed in spades. Money for a new saddle and a horse trailer would be nice—and, of course, a new truck to haul the trailer with. She let the piece of pink paper flutter into her wastebasket. So much for the wisdom of fortune cookies.

She nibbled one half. Stale. She spit it into the wastebasket and tossed in the other half behind it. *There should be a law against giving out stale fortune cookies, let alone stale fortunes.*

She crossed to the window and looked out at the yard she and Gran had worked so hard over. The roses wore their October finery, blooming again after a slowdown in the heat of summer. Pink and red begonias lined the bed at the back of the yard. Carrots rose their feathery plumes in front of the squash, and pumpkins sent tendrils snaking everywhere.

I suppose I could have fun carving jack-o-lanterns with Bobby and Billy. The Double Bs. They and Robert and Lindy always laughed whenever she called them by the name she had given them.

DJ pushed away from the window, full of memories, and slumped into the chair in front of her desk. "Like they really care what I think. Grown-ups don't consider kids at all when they make changes in their lives." She hung her head in her hands. If only she could call Amy, or better yet, Gran. But Gran wasn't home, and Amy's mother had a rule against phone calls after eight.

Could this be defined as an emergency? DJ shook her head, defeat setting around her shoulders like a lead cape. Opening her algebra book to the assigned page, she began her homework. "If x equals blank and y is twenty-four, what is . . ." DJ snapped her pencil in two. What did it matter? She slammed the book shut and stuffed it into her backpack.

Taking out her drawing pad and number-three charcoal pencil, she crossed to the bed and made a nest against the headboard with her pillows. Finally, with the pad propped on her knees, she closed her eyes. That way, it was easier to picture Major.

After a few moments of concentration, she began drawing. Five minutes later, she tore off the first sheet. The sketch looked more like a camel. The next one closely resembled an okapi. She dumped the pad onto the floor before she wasted any more paper.

Once in bed, comforted by her Mickey Mouse nightshirt, she tried to pray. Gran had always said to pray when you were stuck—it was even better if you prayed before you got stuck in the first place. But then, Gran found it easy to ask God for things. He really answered her.

DJ thumped her pillows into submission and turned onto her side.

"God, help! I don't want a new father—I don't even know the one I've got. Please, please, *please,* don't let Mom and Robert get married. Mom and I . . . we . . . well, we're just starting to get along as it is. What am I gonna do now?" She waited. There was no answer. She heard footsteps coming up the stairs, so she shut off the light and rolled onto her side to face the wall.

"DJ?" Mom tapped at the closed door. When there was only silence, her feet padded down the hall to her own room.

DJ heard her mother's bedroom door click shut. Lindy was a strong believer in privacy, both for herself and her daughter. Right now, the daughter felt . . . DJ tried to figure out how she felt.

Lost seemed as good a word as any.

"Close your mouth, Ames, you'll catch flies."

"But you say your mother and Robert—?" Amy stopped, heedless of the students milling around them. She ignored the one who bumped into her, and kept her attention riveted on DJ.

"Bummer, huh?" DJ kicked her sneakers against the curb.

"Well, maybe not."

"Where's your head, girl? I'm counting on you to help me break this fast romance into a thousand pieces."

"What does Gran say?"

DJ kicked again. "I don't know. I haven't talked with her. She was gone last night." She raised her head. "There's the bell. We'll have to discuss this later. Try to come up with a really creative idea in the meantime. A plan—you know, the kind that's so good they'll think they thought of it."

"Right." Amy's groan rose clear from her ankles. "You know what happens to our good ideas."

"Not this time. This time I'm desperate." DJ slung her backpack over one shoulder and headed for the doorway.

"When aren't you?" Amy had to take three strides to DJ's two.

"But this time . . . this time could mean the difference between . . ." DJ wrinkled her brow. Life and death sounded too—well, *normal* would do for lack of a better word. She skidded into her homeroom just as the final bell rang.

The house smelled empty, the same lonely smell that greeted DJ every day now. Would she never stop missing Gran? As she climbed the stairs to her room, she remembered the way fresh-baked cookie perfume had floated out to the street to greet her. If Gran had been too involved in painting to bake, a familiar turpentine and oil scent had said she was hard at work. The easel set up in the corner of the family room had always exhibited the artwork for the latest children's book Gran was illustrating, the stereo playing one of Gran's "uplifting" tapes.

So many times, DJ had teased Gran about her music when they both knew DJ enjoyed listening to the contemporary Christian singers as much as her grandmother.

DJ reminded herself that Gran lived only a mile and a half away and she could drop in to experience all those things if she wanted to. Frequently she did—but only after her work at the Academy and only on nights when her mother said she'd be home late.

DJ did her usual quick-change routine and clattered back down the stairs, leaving the memories behind. The answering machine winked its red eye at her. She pushed the play button to hear her mother's voice. "Please be ready to go to dinner by 7:15. We will be going someplace nice, so make sure you are presentable."

DJ read between the lines. Presentable meant "take a shower so you don't smell like horse." But who did the "we" refer to? Would it be just the two of them? The entire family? Was Robert coming? The tone said her mother had a long way to go before she would be happy with her one and only daughter.

If DJ was going to be clean and dressed by 7:15, she'd better hit warp speed right about now. She grabbed a soda and an apple from the refrigerator, a food bar from the cupboard, and stuck her cereal bowl and glass from that morning in the dishwasher. No sense adding fuel to her mother's fire. Everything had better be put away.

DJ rushed out the door and hopped onto her bike. "Put a move on it," she called as she coasted past Amy. "Her highness called and said to be ready tonight for dinner out."

"Well, at least she won't yell at you while you're in public." Amy pedaled up beside her friend.

"Hope not. She read somewhere that restaurants are perfect for having heavy discussions—people are on their best behavior." DJ alternately munched and sipped as she pedaled until they reached the steep part of the hill where she needed two hands to steer. "You come up with any great ideas?"

"For what?"

"Getting this wedding canceled, of course. What did you think I meant?"

"DJ, I hate to remind you, but all our great ideas flop, remember?" Amy halted at the stop sign. "Besides, Robert is a nice man. And personally, I think having a father around is the best."

"Yeah, but you've got a good one."

"I know. Anyway, I think you should let nature take its course."

"Nature what? Are you out of your mind?" DJ skidded in the loose gravel, then dismounted. They both parked their bikes in the shade of the long barn containing four rows of stalls. DJ finished her soda in a gulp and dropped the can in a recycling barrel as they trotted across the dusty parking lot to the office. Once inside the dim interior, they looked up at the roster, a shiny white board with names and duties written in erasable marker.

"Yuck." Amy pointed at the name Tony Andrada. Recently relocated from the South, Tony had already made a name for himself as one of the most disliked student workers at the Academy. He gave a new and deeper meaning to the term *redneck*.

"Well, at least I don't have to work with him. James was bad enough."

Together they turned and entered Bridget's office. A stack of bills, invoices, magazines, and advertisements teetered on the edge of the desk, nearly hiding the woman working at a pullout board.

"Just do not sneeze in here, and I will remain calm." Bridget looked up from glaring at a ledger. "Is either one of you skilled enough on a computer to enter all this information for me so I can finally get organized?"

Both girls shook their heads. "Sorry."

"Me too. Oh, DJ, Angie's mother called. Angie had another bad asthma attack last night, and they kept her overnight at the hospital. She will not be here for her lesson today."

"Fiddle." DJ rubbed a finger over the scar from a childhood burn on her right palm. "She's the best rider of the group, and the one with real natural talent. If only she didn't have to miss so much."

"Actually, we are fortunate to have her at all. Many parents would say riding is off limits to an asthmatic child due to the dust. The Lincolns trust us a lot to let her ride here."

"After she got stung by the bee up in the park, I'd want to keep her in sight all the time." DJ flinched at the memory. "Seeing her gasping for breath like that and having to give her a shot scared me half to death."

"You did well." Bridget cocked her head and studied the two girls. "You all right, DJ?"

"Sorta."

"Well, if you need a friendly ear, I have two." Bridget paused as if giving DJ a chance to add something. "Okay, this is not written on the board, but since Angie is not coming to care for her horse, could you find a few minutes to ride him or at least put him on the hot walker? And, Amy, Tony got here late, so he needs some help grooming the horses along the north wall. Hilary will not be coming, so I would like you to supervise him." Bridget raised a hand to forestall any groaning on their part. "I know Tony is a bit of a pain, but he will become accustomed to our ways. He *is* a good rider."

But if he treats his horse like he treats us, it doesn't matter how good a rider he is, DJ thought. *He'll be out of here. And it won't be a moment too soon*. "Anything else?" DJ fingered the scar again. She'd found herself doing that more often lately—at least it beat chewing her fingernails.

Bridget looked up at the clock above the duty board. "I have a new client coming in a half hour. I might be late for your jumping lesson, DJ, but feel free to start without me."

"Sure." DJ bit her lower lip. "I have to leave at 6:30 so . . ."

"So you may have a shorter lesson today. We will make up for it later." Bridget glanced at the stack before her. "If a wind came through here, we would have a paper snowstorm. Something has to be done about this." She bent her head to her task, one yellow pencil stuck above her ear in her slicked-back hair.

DJ and Amy trotted back across the parking lot and into the tack room for grooming buckets. "Go ahead, say it, Ames." DJ's chuckle had just the right amount of fiendish glee.

"My mother would wash my mouth out with soap."

"I'm not your mother."

"But once I got started, I wouldn't stop. That . . . that . . ."

"Yes, go on." DJ made beckoning motions with her hands.

" . . . that absolute jerk!"

"Hmm . . . not good enough—or bad enough, in this case. We called James 'The Jerk,' remember? We need to be a little more creative around here."

"Beat it, DJ, I've got work to do." Amy flipped another soft brush into her bucket and headed down the sandy aisle between rows of box stalls.

DJ checked her watch. Only a half hour till the students in her beginners' class arrived. She grabbed a bridle that she knew would fit Angie's horse and hurried across the middle lane to where the gelding was stabled. Within minutes, she had him groomed, tacked, and out in the ring. He was an easy-gaited horse, and DJ enjoyed the exercise as much as he did. She put him through his paces, all the things she'd been teaching the girls: walk, jog, lope, reverses, figure eights, back ups, and stops and starts.

"How come you have Angie's horse out here?" Krissie, a bubbly little blonde, rode into the arena.

"Angie had a bad attack." DJ reined her mount to the center of the ring. "How about if I teach from horseback?"

"Fine with me."

"Me too." Sam, short for Samantha, followed Krissie into the ring. They both walked their horses to the left and stayed just off the rail like they'd been taught.

"We're going to be adding another rider to this class soon," DJ announced, keeping her reins steady and patting the gelding's neck. At their unison groans, she raised her voice. "Hey, let's give the poor guy a chance when he comes.

"Now focus. Jog, please."

By the time the lesson was done, the gelding was tired of standing still. DJ rode over to the gate. "You did fine. Krissie, what do you think about working toward entering the trail-riding class? Both you and your horse are calm enough for that." She turned. "Sam, you have to keep an even pace. You move fast one minute, then slow the next—makes me wonder who's giving the orders."

"My horse is. He's bigger."

Sam and Krissie laughed but cut it short when DJ frowned at them.

"I'm trying—really I am." Sam looked sheepish. "I will do better. I'll practice between now and next week. We'll do it right. You'll see."

"That's better. No 'trys' allowed here." DJ let her smile return. "You done good."

How many times had she had to replace "I'll try" with "I will" back when she was first beginning? Everyone started out saying "I'll try" at first. And trying wasn't good enough at the Academy. "Now hustle. I see your moms waiting."

While the girls took care of their horses, DJ put Angie's horse up and groomed Patches, the gelding she was training for the Johnsons. The horse had come in green broke, and the owners had no idea how to make him mind. Now Mrs. Johnson was finally able to take riding lessons on Patches.

Fortunately, Bridget had talked the Johnsons into giving their son riding lessons on a pony at first. The boy, Andrew, acted scared to death of horses in general and

Patches in particular. Soon he would be DJ's private pupil every Wednesday. So far, he hadn't been on Bandit yet, but at least he was grooming him. DJ already felt like she was winning.

Just as she'd suspected, her own riding lesson was cut short, but she almost didn't mind because she couldn't keep her mind on jumping. As dinnertime grew closer, DJ fought to think about something else—anything other than her mother and Robert and their crazy engagement.

Bridget made her repeat the lower jumps over and over.

"I know, I know—my focus is shot to pieces." DJ stopped herself at Bridget's sharp look. Grumbling would do no good.

3

"DJ, I'M SPEAKING TO YOU." Lindy wore the tight-lipped look that meant trouble lay just over the horizon.

DJ looked up from the circles she was drawing on the white tablecloth with the tines of her fork. "I know. I heard you."

"Then why didn't you answer?"

"I don't know what to say."

"You have to admit that was an honest answer." Robert placed a hand on Lindy's arm.

Lindy jerked her arm away and brushed a strand of hair from her cheek.

DJ saw hurt in Robert's eyes.

Mister, you ain't seen nothin' yet. Wait till she has PMS. DJ had to fight to keep a grin off her face. She didn't need a creative idea to break this romance up, she just needed to keep quiet.

A woman dressed in a black evening gown played a harp by the velvet curtains.

"Can I get you something else, sir?" A white-jacketed waiter appeared at Robert's elbow.

"No . . . ah . . ." Robert looked from Lindy to DJ. "Would either of you care for dessert?"

DJ started to shake her head, then changed her mind.

"Could I see the dessert tray, please?" She made the request as smoothly as if she ate at places like this every other Tuesday. She tried to ignore the withering look from her mother, but she could feel it digging into her scalp.

Robert had discarded three different conversational topics by the time the New York cheesecake with blueberry topping arrived.

"Want a bite, Mom?" DJ offered with a smile.

"No, thank you." The *k* could have cut glass.

"So, Robert, what do the twins think of this idea of yours?" DJ ventured.

"The twins?" Robert had obviously resorted to polite smiles that hid his real thoughts.

"You know, Bobby and Billy." DJ savored the last bite of cheesecake. She felt as though she was going to be sick. She hadn't eaten this much at one time since who knew when.

"They think that having a new mom and a big sister would be the best thing since ice cream."

"If you are finished, Darla Jean, I would like to go now." Lindy shot DJ an icy look.

"Yes, thank you. I'm done." DJ carefully folded her napkin and set it on the table. "Thank you, Robert, for the awesome dinner."

Robert pushed back his chair and stood to pull out Lindy's for her. "Honey, are you all right?"

Honey? Gag time again. DJ followed her mother out the door, Robert bringing up the rear. By the time the valet brought the car around, Lindy was rubbing her temples.

Headache—big time. DJ recognized the signs. An itty-bitty twinge of guilt waved to get her attention, but DJ deliberately faced the other way. She hadn't said one wrong thing. In fact, she'd hardly said anything at all. But if looks could kill, she'd been skewered.

So that was the new rule: Don't answer even when spoken to—until the third time or when the tone took on a real bite. Ignore, ignore, ignore.

But when DJ crawled into bed after faking polite goodnights, all she could think of was how disappointed her Gran would have been with her that night. DJ rolled over and tried counting horses instead. She thought about the Olympics and being on the Olympic team. But when she finally fell asleep, the feeling that she had somehow let down Gran still troubled her.

"How come I'm more tired now than when I went to bed?" DJ's grumbles received no answers. There was no one to hear them. DJ was beginning to think she was going loony, all this talking to herself. Maybe she should get a dog. At least then there would be someone to listen to her.

Yeah, just like you listened to your mother last night. Where had that thought come from?

The car honking outside told her Mr. Yamamoto and Amy were waiting to take her to school. Wait till Ames heard the plan DJ had come up with before dropping off to sleep. It was destined to work.

"You're going to what?" Amy and DJ hadn't had time to talk in the car without Amy's father overhearing. Now, that afternoon, they were on their way up the hill to the Academy.

"You heard me." DJ took another bite of her apple, tossed the core into the bushes, and pedaled to catch up.

"Yeah, but you—keeping your mouth shut? Gimme a break." Amy's grin took any sting out of her words.

"You'll see." DJ tried to forget today's message on the

red-eyed answering machine at home. Her mother had said, *Tonight, we talk.* Her voice had sounded about as friendly as that of a wounded wolf.

Lindy's headache must have gone away. Or maybe she had gone to work in order to avoid remaining at home with her daughter.

DJ set to grooming her horses for the day, whistling so she didn't have to think. Tonight Gran would be back. That was one thing to put on her things-to-thank-God-for list. Gran and Joe were returning from her yearly trip to New York to talk with her publishers.

DJ stopped picking hooves when a loud voice broke into her reverie.

"I don't have to listen to you." The nasty edge said it could be none other than Tony Andrada.

The answer came as a soft murmur.

DJ listened hard. It had to be Hilary. Why didn't she just tell him to shape up or she'd ship him out to Bridget? He had to listen to Hilary; Bridget had assigned them to each other. Didn't Tony understand that the older student workers trained the new ones? And that they all worked as a team?

The angry voice came from farther away. Tony was heading out to the arena.

"Hilary?" DJ left the horse she was working with and went hunting for her mentor and friend. Hilary Jones had always been one to encourage the younger members, DJ included. Through the years, watching Hilary's graceful riding in the jumping ring had given DJ pure pleasure—and, depending on which day it was, a bad case of envy.

No answer.

"Hilary?" DJ stuck her head into the empty stall. At least she thought it was empty until she saw Hilary sitting in the far corner, her hands between raised knees. A tear meandered down her cocoa-colored cheek.

"Hil, are you all right?"

Hilary wound one corn-row braid around her finger. "I don't think so."

DJ slumped down the wall until she was sitting beside her friend. What could she say? "It's Tony, isn't it?"

"Umm."

"When are you going to talk to Bridget about him?"

"I'm not."

"What?" DJ turned to look the college freshman in the face. Hilary kept her gaze forward. She let the tear drip off her chin.

"DJ, if I tell you something, do you promise not to tell anyone else?"

"Not even Amy?"

"That's up to you." Hilary sighed. "I'm thinking of moving my horse to a different stable."

"Hilary Jones, whatever is the matter with you? You know Bridget is the best coach around. And not only is this the best-run stable, but it's also the one closest to your house."

"I know. But, DJ, this situation with Tony . . . it's a racial thing. He called me a . . . a black . . ." She couldn't finish the sentence.

"You don't have to say it, Hil. I know Tony is a real creep." DJ stared at her hands. This couldn't be happening in Pleasant Hill, California. "But if you move your horse, you let Tony win. You can't do that."

"What else can I do?"

"I don't know, but Amy and I'll think of something. I'll talk to Gran, too." DJ held up a hand. "Don't worry, I won't tell her any names. But you can bet she'll be praying for you, and Gran's prayers always get answers. You wait and see."

"I'll give it till after the fall regional show in the beginning of December. If he doesn't come around by then, I'm out of here." Hilary pushed herself to her feet. "Sorry, DJ, that's the most I can give. I can't let this keep getting in the way of my schoolwork like it has been."

"The show isn't very far away."

"I know." Hilary extended a hand to pull DJ to her feet and stepped out of the stall. She turned back. "You better get out there. Your little student is coming down the aisle looking for you."

DJ groaned. "Hang in there, Hil. We'll turn things around, we will." *I could beat that stupid redneck into the ground if I had to. But I can't do that. What are we gonna do?*

DJ met Andrew halfway up the aisle. "You looking for me?"

Her small pupil tried to smile, but fear darkened his eyes, the same fear she'd seen each week during the time she'd been working with him. Whatever could have happened to make him so afraid? She'd asked his parents, but they insisted that no horse had ever run away with him or lunged at or bitten him or any such thing. DJ and Bridget were both stumped by the situation.

Right now, it was DJ's job to get the boy over his fear since his parents wanted the family to ride together regularly.

"You been to see Bandit?"

Andrew shook his head. He reached for DJ's hand and glued himself to her side. At five feet seven, DJ wasn't a giant, but she felt like one next to this little boy who looked more like eight than ten—and a small eight at that.

"Bandit's waiting to see you. He likes the way you brush his legs."

"Really?" Two huge blue eyes looked up at her.

"Sure, I think you're going to be a very good horse groomer." DJ felt like swinging him up into her arms and hugging his skinny body. She'd always been a sucker for big blue eyes. "How about combing his mane today?"

They stopped in front of the stall, where Bandit pushed his nose over the web gate and nickered silently, his nostrils wide to sniff for treats.

"See, I told you he likes you."

Andrew made like a mollusk and clung.

DJ stroked Bandit's nose, then dug in her pocket for a horse cookie. "You like cookies, Andrew?"

He nodded.

"So does Bandit. These are made especially for horses. Why don't you give it to him? Like this." DJ held part of the cookie on the flat palm of her hand and let Bandit lip it up. "See, it tickles." She took Andrew's hand and tickled the palm. "Feels funny, huh?"

Andrew nodded. A smile almost peeked out of one side of his mouth.

"You want to try?"

He shook his head vigorously, setting the dark hair that flopped over his forehead to swinging. Then he reached down into the grooming bucket and picked up a brush. With a sigh that shook his entire body, he looked up at her. "Please tie him."

"You are one gutsy kid." DJ gave him her most reassuring smile. "What makes you think Bandit will bite you?"

"Horses bite. I've seen it."

"Really?" DJ snapped both crossties to Bandit's halter and opened the web gate. "Where?"

"On TV." Andrew ducked under the ropes, keeping a careful eye on Bandit's head. Standing as far away as possible, he brushed down the gray shoulder.

"Oh, really? What happened?" DJ picked up the other brush and moved to Bandit's far side.

"A horse bit a boy and made him bleed. I saw one trample a lady, too. Horses are mean."

"Do you think Bandit is mean?" Andrew shook his head

and kept on brushing. Bit by bit, he edged closer so he could brush more easily.

DJ kept up a line of chatter, telling Andrew about the times Bandit did well in the show-ring and took children on trail rides. She even got a laugh when she told him about the kids tracking in green horse manure on a woman's brand-new white carpet at one of the birthday parties. The more she got him to talk, the closer he moved to the pony.

After a while, DJ asked, "How about feeding Bandit a treat?"

Silence. Then a soft, "All right."

She reached into her pocket and pulled out a mutilated horse cookie. "Here. If you like, I'll keep my hand right by yours."

Andrew nodded. He held his hand out flat and watched DJ place the cookie on the palm. She put her hand under his and squatted down beside the boy. "Anytime you're ready."

She kept the other hand on Bandit's halter just in case he moved too quickly. "Easy, Bandit. Go ahead, Andrew, talk to Bandit and tell him what you are going to do. Horses like to hear our voices."

"B-Bandit. I have a c-cookie for you." Andrew stepped closer and held the treat out just like DJ had shown him. Bandit opened his eyes, blinked, and lipped the goodie, his whiskers scraping the boy's palm.

"He tickles." Andrew's grin could have lit the entire barn on a gray day. But just at that moment, Bandit stamped his foot and flicked his tail to chase a pesky fly.

Andrew leaped back, tripped over the bucket, and sprawled in the straw. He scrambled to his feet and was out of the stall before DJ had time to blink. She could hear him crying as he went.

"Bummer. Double bummer." She untied the pony and

picked up the brushes scattered in the fall. *Better luck next time—if there is a next time. Poor kid.*

Later when she told Mrs. Johnson about the conversation, the woman shook her head.

"I had no idea. Why, Andrew knows those things on television aren't real. We've certainly talked about it often enough."

DJ just looked at her.

"But that's why he's so afraid, huh?" Mrs. Johnson sighed. "Guess I better pay more attention—he's such a sensitive child. Thanks, DJ."

The rest of the day continued the downhill slide. Patches acted as though he'd been snacking on loco weed. DJ had to return to the basics of stop, start, walk, and jog. She refused to let him tear around the ring like he wanted. And Angie's horse had to be worked again, too. The poor girl was still in the hospital.

"They are trying out a new routine," Bridget said when DJ questioned her. "They are hoping it could stop some of the attacks."

"I sure hope so." DJ resolved to create a card for Angie that night. She knew how down she would feel if she were in that hospital bed.

Major behaved in his usual easygoing manner, but as dusk fell, DJ's thoughts kept returning to what was waiting for her at home. After less than an hour of working Major, she finally put her horse away. It wasn't his fault she couldn't concentrate. It was a good thing tonight wasn't a lesson night because DJ knew she would have been scolded. She was doing a pretty fair job of that herself.

You know better than this, DJ. Now concentrate. A true rider puts everything out of her mind but the horse and the jumps. But the reminders didn't help. Telling herself that all she had to do tonight was keep quiet didn't help either. Staying silent in a restaurant with Robert present was one thing. But one on one with her mother was something else entirely.

The clipped voice on the answering machine replayed itself in her head. *Tonight, we talk*.

4

HER MOTHER'S CAR SAT IN THE DRIVEWAY.

Thanks a bunch, God. Why didn't you make her work late tonight? I hoped you were on my side. DJ parked her bike by the driver's side of the car and opened the door so she could push the garage opener. The garage door did its usual moaning and groaning routine on its way up. It would have been nice for it to be quiet this one time. Then maybe DJ could have sneaked in, parked her bike, and tiptoed up to her room without her mother knowing.

"Yeah, and maybe the sky will fall." She grumbled at her bike when the kickstand didn't go down on the first flip.

The back door squeaked when she opened it. Her boots sounded like hammers on the kitchen floor no matter how lightly she tried to step.

"I'm in the living room."

Uh-oh. Trouble! DJ felt herself freeze. Here it came. She peered around the corner. Her mother sat in a corner of the sofa, her legs crossed over the middle cushion. She'd changed from her work suit into an emerald lounging outfit. A half-empty glass of sparkling water dripped moisture on the coaster protecting the oak end table.

Her mother had been home for some time.

"Come on in."

"You want me to change first?" DJ knew the rules. Jeans scented with horse were not allowed in the living room.

"Of course."

On the way upstairs, DJ tried to decipher her mother's tone. Angry? She shucked off her jeans and tossed them into the hamper. Furious? Her T-shirt followed. Hurt? She grabbed a pair of shorts from the drawer and a clean T-shirt, this one with a leaping dolphin on the front. Gran had bought it for DJ on her honeymoon cruise.

If only Gran were here. Of course, she'd want me to apologize. But this isn't my fault.

DJ could hear Gran's voice as clearly as if she were right here in the room. "Any time you hurt someone else, you must ask forgiveness and apologize." Then Gran would follow her pronouncement with a Bible verse. How could DJ argue with the Bible?

She reminded herself again that this whole mess wasn't her fault. All she'd done was keep her mouth shut. Hadn't she been told to do that a million times by now?

She entered the darkened room and took the wing chair across from her mother. Silence reigned. The light from a crystal lamp on an end table made a halo around Lindy's head. Her mother appeared to be studying the painting on the wall, one of Gran's.

DJ knew it by heart. Gran had painted it of DJ in the garden when her granddaughter was five and loved sniffing the roses, especially the pink ones. The picture had won an award at the county fair. The judge had said the painting had the luminescent quality of French Impressionism. DJ had been wearing a floppy straw hat and a polka-dot sunsuit that Gran had sewn for her granddaughter's fifth birthday. Gran had kept the sunsuit, and DJ had proudly pinned the hat to her bedroom wall.

The silence between mother and daughter stretched like a rubber band pulled to its limit.

DJ sat on her fingers to keep from chewing her nails. *Just holler at me and get this over with,* she wanted to say.

"What are we going to do, Darla Jean?" Her mother's voice held all the sadness of a wounded puppy.

"Mom, I didn't murder anyone or anything." The hoped-for light tone fell flatter than a flour tortilla.

Lindy looked across the space between them, a space that at that moment seemed to measure the width of the Pacific Ocean.

"Mom, it's not my fault. All I did was . . ." The words trailed off. If only DJ could make like a slug and slime her way out of the room. Her thumbnail ached to be chewed on.

"No, it's not your fault. But you hurt someone who doesn't deserve to be hurt."

DJ immediately knew who she meant. "Robert?"

"Yes." Lindy kept her gaze trained on her daughter's face.

If DJ concentrated on not chewing her fingernail, maybe she could make it through this tortured conversation.

"He had the silly idea that we would make a good family. He says he fell in love not only with me, but with you." Each word dropped like a tear.

Why couldn't they yell at each other like they usually did? DJ felt as if a giant hand was shoving her deep into the chair. "I . . . I'm sorry."

"I know. I can tell. Sometimes sorry just isn't enough." Lindy leaned forward. "Listen to me carefully, Darla Jean. You keep saying you want me to treat you like an adult, that you are growing up. Well, I tried to do that, and you blew it. You blew it big time." She sighed. "Robert says we'll work this out in time. But I don't know." Her mother shook her head. "I just don't know."

DJ curled her feet under her and tried to disappear into

the back of the chair. She couldn't think of a thing to say.

She went to bed feeling like she'd kicked a floppy-eared puppy.

The next night, since her mother had to attend a graduate course, DJ waved goodbye to Amy and turned left toward Gran and Joe's. She'd have dinner with them, then Joe would drive her home. If you could call the icebox she'd left behind home, that is. Even with the air-conditioner off, the temperature must have registered only thirty degrees. There had been no message from her mother.

DJ pedaled up to her grandmother's new house. She and Joe had lived there little more than a month and already she could tell it was Gran's house. Roses bloomed by the door, and a flowering bougainvillea vine painted the adjoining garage brilliant purple. Best of all, the smell of fresh chocolate chip cookies met DJ's nostrils as she mounted the three concrete steps. Pots of pink begonias were in a race to outbloom one another on each step.

"Gran?"

"In here, darlin'." All the years of living in California still hadn't erased Gran's soft Southern drawl. Like Gran's gentle hands, the accent meant love in DJ's mind. Her Gran always loved everyone, no matter what.

DJ followed her nose into the kitchen. "You have green paint on your chin," she teased as she gave her grandmother a hug and snitched a cookie off the counter. She turned to greet the man sitting at the round table in the bay window overlooking the backyard. "Hi, Joe." She grinned around the cookie-crumble greeting. "I was beginning to think you guys were never coming home."

"Hi, yourself. Hand me one of those, will you? Melanie's

been keeping me on diet restrictions." He tried to sound abused and failed miserably.

"After all we ate in New York, I shouldn't be baking at all." Gran slid the last cookies off the sheet and set it in the sink. She turned off the oven, arranged cookies on a plate, and brought it with her to the table. "Do you want anything to drink, DJ?"

DJ shook her head. "Might spoil my dinner."

Gran laughed and poked DJ on the shoulder. "Fat chance. So, do you want to tell me what's going on?"

Leave it to Gran to get right to the point.

"Nothing much. Major and I are getting better every day, and school—well, school is school."

"Have you heard anything about your drawing yet?"

"Nope. In another couple of weeks. How come it takes so long to judge a bunch of drawings?"

"Depends on how many entries they had." Gran took a bite of cookie and leveled one of her let's-get-to-the-point looks at her granddaughter. "What else?"

"Well, Robert wants to marry Mom."

"And . . ." the soft voice prompted.

"Do *you* think it's a good idea?"

"Not my place to say."

"Did you know about it?" DJ moved her gaze from Gran to Joe and back again.

"It seemed like a good possibility." Joe joined the conversation.

"Why didn't someone warn me?" DJ slumped in her chair. "I *hate* surprises." She stuck one finger in her mouth and bit off the cuticle. With a guilty look at Gran, DJ picked up another cookie. "I have been doing better—about chewing my fingernails, that is." She sighed. Gran was much too good at waiting for answers. "Gran, this thing between Robert and Mom isn't my fault. All I did was—well, nothing."

"That's not like you."

"I know. It drove Mom crazy. Me too, nearly. I wanted to yell at her." DJ studied the bloody spot on her chewed cuticle. Nobody moved. No one said anything. "You should be proud of me for not losing my temper."

"Are you?"

DJ grimaced and shook her head. "But think about this: My mother is having enough trouble taking care of me—what will she do with twin boys?" She looked up. "You could always come home."

"I *am* home." Gran smiled across the table at Joe and reached for his hand.

Joe leaned forward. "DJ, you didn't ask for my opinion, but I'm going to give it to you anyway. Now, I might be prejudiced a bit, but my son Robert is a fine man." He looked to Gran for agreement. At her nod, he continued. "You could do far worse for a father than him." He leaned forward. "In fact, your life might be a lot easier."

"With the Double Bs?" DJ's look of horror made both adults laugh.

"They are a handful, I admit, but Robert makes them mind. And I know he cares deeply for your mother."

"Don't you think it's time she had a man's love in her life?" Gran stood and rested a hand on her granddaughter's shoulder. "You need to do some praying about this."

"I knew you'd say that." DJ flopped back and crossed her arms over her chest. "And if I know you, you're going to find me a Bible verse to learn, too. One I can't even argue with. That's just not fair."

"Maybe it's time you found your own verse." Gran leaned against Joe's solid shoulder. Her eyes twinkled, and the smile on her face made DJ yearn for the mornings she'd come down to the family room to find Gran in her chair, Bible on her lap and a ready smile for a sleepy girl. There had already been so much change in DJ's life. How could she stand any more?

DJ propped her elbows on the table. "Maybe. Are we going to eat soon? I'm starved."

"Not enough cookies?" Joe raised his hands in horror. "Melanie, quick! Feed the child."

It still seemed so strange to hear Gran called by her first name. Everyone else called her Gran or Mother. DJ got to her feet. "You want me to help?"

By the time they finished off the meatloaf and baked potatoes, DJ knew she had to hurry to her homework. When she mentioned it to Joe, he rose to his feet right away.

"And here I thought we could have a relaxing evening, just the three of us. I found a couple of ads in a horse magazine about a cutting horse." Joe took his jacket out of the hall closet as he spoke. "Maybe this weekend we can go look at a couple of them."

"Where?" DJ set her dishes in the sink and wrapped an arm around her grandmother.

"Up by Redding. Melanie said she'd like to go. We could make a day of it."

"We could leave after I'm done working at the Academy. I need to spend some extra time with Patches. He's been a brat lately. Ever since Mrs. Johnson started riding him, he thinks he can get away with murder." DJ dropped a kiss on Gran's cheek. "Thanks for the yummy dinner. Maybe we could stop on the way at that gourmet olive place and get a couple of jars. Mom loves their spicy ones."

"Buying your way back into her good graces?" Gran patted DJ's cheek. "God will work this all out, you'll see, darlin'."

That night, DJ didn't have to worry about arguing with her mother. The frosty message on the machine said she would be home late, well after DJ's bedtime. Her mother was finally near completing her master's degree in business administration. The last assignment, to write a thesis, already had her tied in knots, and she hadn't even decided on a topic. DJ didn't know what it would be like to have her mother *not* going to school.

She wished she'd asked to spend the night at Gran's.

Why is it that when you're bummed about one thing, it makes other things bummers, too? DJ forgot her assignment at home, and when she called to see if Gran or Joe could bring it into school for her, they were out. More than once she envied kids who could call home for something and have their mothers bring it. It used to be that way at her house, too—even though Gran had promised only one errand a quarter. That way, DJ had learned to be responsible for her own things. Until today, anyway.

She glared at her reflection in the mirror. Add a bad hair day on to that and a pop quiz in history and now, by the end of the day, she felt like crawling under a rock, or at least the covers. DJ looked longingly at her unmade bed. All she could remember of her short-on-sleep night was a nightmare where her mother had kept calling her. The voice had faded away every time DJ tried to find her.

She jerked the covers in place, changed clothes, and straightened her bathroom. No sense in adding fuel to a fire ready to burst into flame any time now.

By the time DJ had groomed four horses and cleaned

Major's stall, she felt more like herself. "We'll ride in a while," she assured the rangy bay, who loved to decorate her T-shirts with deep red and white hairs by rubbing his forehead on her chest. DJ gave him an extra bit of carrot and, with another hug, slipped out the gate. Work before pleasure—and Patches had definitely become more work than pleasure.

"You know, you are the most stubborn horse I've ever met." DJ kept the showy dark brown horse to a walk. She'd let him work off steam on the hot walker, then trotted forty-six times—at least it felt that way—around the arena. Still he couldn't seem to mind. Slow jog wasn't in his plan for the day, and his trot left her less than pleased since she was riding Western. Posting made for a less pounding ride. Was Patches picking up on her bad day, or was he just born ornery?

She pulled him to a stop for the umpteenth time. When he finally quit shifting from one foot to the other, she signaled him forward again. Four paces of pounding front hooves, and he was back to a stop. And until he behaved and did as he was told, she couldn't put him away.

"What'd you feed him, Jose?" She reined the snorting gelding over to the fence, where the head stable hand leaned on the aluminum bar watching her. Jose Guerrera, who blamed the gray in his black hair on the antics of the academy kids, had worked at the Academy since long before DJ joined the student workers.

"Just the usual. I put him on the hot walker when I cleaned his stall this morning and left him there a good, long time. He needs a lot of exercise, that one. Pretty hyper."

"Tell me about it." DJ kept the reins taut but stood in her stirrups to stretch her legs. She could see her girls gathering for their class. "Did Mrs. Johnson show up for her lesson?"

Jose shook his head. "Not that I know."

Jose pretty much knew everything that went on around the Academy.

"Okay, rotten horse, once more around. And this time, do what I say."

For some reason, Patches finally minded her. With his ears pricked instead of flat against his head, he walked, jogged, and was eventually allowed to lope. DJ extended the time to several circuits around the ring since both of them could enjoy it now. By the time she'd returned the gelding to the barn, unsaddled him, brushed out the sweaty area under the saddle, and given him half a horse cookie, her girls were already in the ring.

"Hey, Angie, glad to see you back." DJ locked the gate behind her and strode to the center of the arena.

"Thanks. I'm glad to be here."

"Is the new routine helping?"

"Got me. But the hospital is the pits. I kept thinking of you guys out here riding and felt like sneaking away."

"I know the feeling." DJ greeted the others and ordered the lesson to begin. Today if all went well, they would work on backing up.

She led Angie to the middle to show her what she'd already taught the others. Suddenly, a girl let out a shriek.

DJ spun around just in time to see Krissie catapult through the air and land flat out in the sand.

OUT OF THE CORNER OF HER EYE, DJ saw a cat streak across the arena.

Krissie lay without moving while her horse tore around the ring.

DJ dropped to her knees beside the fallen girl. With one hand, she smoothed back the gritty hair that straggled from under her student's riding helmet.

Krissie groaned and rolled over, clutching her stomach. "I . . . I can't breathe." The words came in jerks, so soft DJ could barely hear them.

"Do you hurt anywhere else?" DJ did a visual check. No twisted limbs. Body had landed flat out. She knew what was wrong. "You ever had your breath knocked out of you before?"

"Is she okay?" Bridget appeared at DJ's side and knelt by the fallen rider.

"Wind's knocked out of her." DJ kept a gentle hand on Krissie's now rising and falling rib cage. "You're gonna make it, kid. Now you know what a real fall feels like."

"Yeah . . . awful." Krissie's eye's widened. "Where's my horse? Is he okay?"

"Spoken like a true horsewoman." Bridget sank back on her heels. "Jose will have caught your horse in a few minutes. You did not by any chance feed him before riding? Jose is trying to lure him with grain."

"No." Krissie sat up, with a little help from DJ. "Whew, that scared me."

"I bet it did." DJ stood and pulled Krissie to her feet. "Now you know why I keep telling all of you to pay attention to your horse and what's going on around you. If you'd seen the cat before your horse did, you'd have grabbed the reins and the horn and been ready to move with him."

"Instead of smacking the ground." Sam had been the one to dismount and dash across to the office for Bridget. She stood now with her horse's reins in one hand, the other patting her mount's neck. "Boy, I thought you were a goner."

Krissie brushed sand off her stomach and chest and spit out still more. "This ground felt mighty hard for being soft sand." She took a couple of steps and spit again.

"Here's your horse, missy." Jose handed Krissie the reins. "He likes extra feed as much as anyone."

"Thanks." Krissie glared at her horse and started leading him toward the gate.

"Where are you going?" DJ asked.

"To put him away." Krissie looked back over her shoulder.

DJ shook her head. "Not yet. We have a lesson to finish. Mount up and join the others." She made a circling motion with her hand, letting the girls know they should ride to the left.

"But . . . but . . . I still have dirt in my teeth." Krissie glanced down at her dirty clothes. "I . . ." She glared at DJ. "I want to go home."

"You'll be home soon enough. Now get back on your horse, and let's finish this lesson. Your mother isn't even here yet." DJ's tone allowed no room for argument.

Krissie looked at her now quiet horse. He stood still,

head hanging. She sucked in a deep breath as if gathering courage, glared at DJ one more time, muttered something, and took the reins. She slipped a booted foot into the stirrup and swung aboard.

"Congratulations, I'm proud of you."

"For what?" Krissie adjusted the reins and squeezed her heels into her horse's sides. He moved forward as though nothing had happened.

"For getting right back on. Tomorrow it would have been harder." DJ turned to the others and signaled for them to change directions. "Okay, move into a lope."

DJ sucked in a deep breath.

"Good job," Bridget's voice startled her. DJ had forgotten her teacher was still watching behind her. "You are an excellent teacher for one your age. Besides being a fine rider."

DJ felt as if she'd been given an Olympic gold medal, Bridget's compliments were so rare. "Thank you. I was scared spitless. She could have really gotten hurt."

"Accidents happen, but falls are one of the reasons we keep the sand worked frequently. If one has to learn to fall—and you must admit, no one becomes a good horsewoman without falling a few times—a soft arena is the best place to do it."

"Getting your wind knocked out of you sure is scary."

"It is. But the only student here that would be a real problem for is Angie. It might send her into an asthma attack." Bridget touched DJ's arm. "See you later."

After the lesson, DJ stopped the girls at the gate before allowing them to care for their horses. "Today, you all had a good lesson on how important it is to concentrate on what you are doing. Horses will shy at the littlest things, sometimes even a shadow. You've got to be alert. You'll get better with time. The more you ride, the more ready your body will be to move with the horse when he startles."

"Instead of falling off, like me." Krissie could already laugh about it.

"That's right. And if you take gymnastics at school, you'll learn the safest way to fall. Tucking your head and rolling is better than landing flat out. Now get moving, your moms are waiting."

DJ opened the gate. "Oh, I'll need entry forms for the show next Tuesday. I expect you all to enter three classes this time."

After checking their gear and horses, answering their mothers' questions, and praising Krissie to her worried mother, DJ felt as if she'd earned a lesson on Major. On her way to the gelding's stall, she paused. The words coming from a stall in the other aisle burned her ears. Who was Tony cussing at now? Instead of going to investigate, she quickly saddled Major and mounted outside the barn door. She sat for a moment, not believing what she had just heard. People didn't talk that way around the Academy. Hilary hadn't been making Tony out to be worse than he was, that was sure.

As DJ rode out to the jumping arena, she promised herself that she and Amy would come up with a plan—a plan to make Tony leave the Academy.

That made two plans for her to carry out: One to get rid of Tony, and one to keep Robert from marrying her mother. She and Amy certainly had plenty of work ahead of them. She forced the problems out of her mind and concentrated on her horse. It wouldn't be too cool if she got dumped like Krissie had just because she wasn't paying close enough attention.

DJ warmed up Major so he wouldn't sustain an injury. At the same time, she reviewed his show-ring skills so she could enter him in equitation classes. Like her students, she wanted to be able to enter a minimum of three classes—and at least one of those would be in jumping. DJ had yet to take a first, even in the training shows they sponsored here at Briones Riding Academy. They had one more training show here before the big show in Danville in December.

She focused on keeping Major's strides as even as a metronome's tick, no matter what gait they were in. Walk, trot, canter—all at a controlled pace that showed beautifully. "Good boy." She patted Major's neck and smoothed the lock of mane that insisted on flopping to the left. It wouldn't matter in the ring. She planned to braid his mane with ribbons for the big show.

DJ wished she had someone else to work with so she could see how Major would do with other horses in the ring. But because her horse had learned to ignore distractions during his time on the mounted police force, she knew he would be fine. He had been last time, his first time out.

"Are you ready?" Bridget passed through the narrow gate into the jumping arena.

"Sure am." DJ wanted to tell Bridget what she'd heard Tony say but tattling wasn't allowed. Anyway, DJ had never been a tattler. She set Major into a two-point trot around the ring and over the cavalletti. Every class began with a review of the basics. Sometimes DJ wondered if she'd ever move beyond them.

Bridget adjusted the bars on the two middle jumps. "Now remember—all your aids work as one. Do not rush the jumps."

DJ did exactly as Bridget told her not to.

"Fiddle." She'd been practicing just this, and as soon as Bridget walked into the ring, her hard-earned skills disappeared.

"Good job, DJ," Bridget said at the end of the hour. "I can tell how hard you are working, but remember, people do not learn to jump in a month or a year. Be patient."

DJ replayed the advice as she rode back to the barn. *Be patient*. Easily said—hard to do.

"What an afternoon!" Amy met her by their bikes.

"Did you run into Tony?"

"No, but I heard you made Krissie get right back on after she went down." Amy slung one leg over the seat of her blue ten-speed.

"Yeah, right. You know Bridget's rule: Always get back on unless you are broken or bleeding."

"Hurts bad enough getting the wind knocked out of you."

"Don't I know it."

Together they pedaled up the road to Reliez. At the stop sign, DJ planted both feet on the ground. "Ames, we have to come up with some plans."

Amy groaned. "DJ, you know what happens when we make plans."

"We need two of them. Two big-time plans."

"Do I dare ask what for now?" Amy turned to look at her friend.

DJ frowned. "Tony Andrada, for one. My mother and Robert, for two. We need to force Tony out of the Academy and stop the wedding."

"Not asking much, are you?"

"Ames, this is really important."

"Darla Jean Randall, you remember what happened when you last tried to stop a wedding."

"That was different." DJ started peddling.

"Yeah, right."

When they reached Amy's house, DJ hesitated at the curb. "I mean it, Ames. I need help."

Amy sighed. "When do you want to talk?"

"Tomorrow night. Maybe you can sleep over. Then we'll have lots of time to make plans. Remember to ask if it's okay."

When Amy finally nodded, DJ gave her a thumbs-up sign and pedaled off.

Her mother was home, or at least her car was. DJ went through her usual routine, but when she roamed through the house, it had an empty look. Faint traces of her mother's perfume lingered in the air. DJ climbed the stairs. Passing her room, she knocked on her mother's closed door. When no answer came, she opened it a crack, then wider. Immaculate as always, the room was empty.

DJ returned to the kitchen and checked the machine. No messages. No notes on the board. *Strange*. DJ grabbed an apple out of the bowl of fruit on the counter and ambled out the French doors to turn on the sprinklers. They were going to have to hire someone to take care of the yard work if things didn't change around here. Now that Gran was gone, there were weeds in the flower beds and the grass needed mowing. Maybe DJ could get that done on Saturday before Gran and Joe took her with them to Redding.

Back in the house, DJ dished up the remains of the leftover Chinese food and put the plate in the microwave.

When the bell dinged, DJ took her dinner into the family room, curled up in Gran's chair, and picked up a mystery she'd left on the lamp table and began reading. Lost in the adventures of teen sleuth Jennie McGrady, she didn't hear the door open.

Before she could draw into a defensive position, the Double Bs grabbed her knees.

"DJ! We been missing you." The two spoke as one. Two round, identical faces grinned up at her—even their curly blond hair waved the same direction.

"So, how are you two?" DJ set her plate aside and gave them both a hug at the same time.

"Daddy brought pizza."

"You like pizza?"

"How come you's already eating?"

"Daddy, DJ didn't wait for us!"

"Didn't you read the note I left?" Lindy, in jeans, looked like a model.

DJ shook her head. "I checked all over."

"I left it on your bed so you would be sure to see it."

"On my bed? I haven't even been in my room. Why didn't you put it by the phone?"

"DJ. DJ!" The twins pulled at her hands. "Show us your horse pitchurs."

"Can we color?"

DJ tried to answer them, listen to her mother, and greet Robert all at once. She felt like clapping her hands over her ears.

"That's enough, boys." The quiet authority in Robert's voice seemed to penetrate the twins' excitement.

They swiveled around. "But DJ . . ."

"No buts. Come and take your places at the table. In fact, you can help DJ set it."

DJ shot her mother a look. She got to her feet, smiled at the boys, and led them into the dining room. Since when was Robert giving the orders around here? And why should she have to eat? She thought of her plate of Chinese, only half eaten. She *was* still hungry—but that wasn't the point. This wasn't Robert's house.

She dug some paper plates out of the cupboard and handed them to the boys. "One plate each."

"What's to drink?"

"Got me. Ask your father. He seems to know better'n I do what's going on around here."

"Darla Jean Randall!" The hiss came from directly behind her.

DJ felt as if she'd been stabbed. Her mother only called

DJ by her full name when she was really angry. Lindy knew how much her daughter hated the name.

"You will be polite, you hear?"

DJ nodded. She reached up for the glasses. "Did you bring soda to drink?"

"No, Robert says the boys can have milk." Lindy leaned over to check the open fridge. "Oh, we're out."

"Yeah, we're out of lots of things. No one's been to the store."

Lindy planted her hands on her slim hips. "Did you mark it on the list?"

DJ pointed out the check marks on a computerized grocery list stuck to the door with an apple magnet.

"Oh" was all Lindy said.

DJ took down the container of powdered lemonade and began mixing it. "If it's sugar he's worried about, tell him we drink diet stuff." She held up the can. "Sugar free."

DJ took the napkins and forks and headed for the dining room. Knowing her mother, she would probably forget the drinks.

"I'm sorry, DJ, I should have called." Robert took the forks and set them around the table. The Double Bs perched on either side of an empty chair.

"That's okay. I'm always ready for pizza." DJ eyed the two giant-sized pizzas, one loaded with everything, the other topped with Canadian Bacon and pineapple. "And you got my favorites."

"Mine too." He dropped his voice. "Left off the anchovies."

DJ felt the beginnings of a smile tug at her mouth. DJ had never shared her mother's love for anchovies. "Thanks."

"DJ, sit here." Both boys patted the empty seat. "We saved it for you."

"What can I say?" Robert lifted his hands in a shrug.

"They think you're the next best thing to Santa Claus."

Robert waited for all to clasp hands and bow heads. "Bobby, your turn to say grace."

Bobby scrunched his eyes closed. "God is great, God is good . . ."

DJ said it along with him under her breath. Since Gran left, the Randalls hadn't said much grace. Her mother had only done it to appease Gran.

Billy chimed in loudly on the "Amen."

Neither DJ nor Lindy could stay mad through dinner. Laughter erupted, calmed, and erupted again between Robert and the boys. DJ felt as though she was in the first car on a roller-coaster.

"Daddy's gonna buy us a pony."

"No, two ponies."

DJ wished she could tell which twin was talking when. "Can anyone tell these two apart?"

"Most of the time," Robert answered. "But not always. At least, not immediately. I watch for certain clues. I'll teach them to you when we have a few minutes."

There he goes again, as if there are going to be many nights like this. She carefully refrained from looking at her mother. Lindy couldn't tell the twins apart, either, and she didn't like using B & B. The pair got full giggle mileage out of her mistakes.

By the time they'd cleaned up after dinner, DJ excused herself. "I've got a bunch of homework to do." She fended off four small, clutching hands. "Later, guys. Next time we'll draw and color." There she went, acting as if this would become a common occurrence, just like Robert.

Help, Amy, we need a plan—and quick!

6

"BUT, AMES, THIS TIME'LL BE DIFFERENT. I promise."

Amy shook her head and sighed. "That's what you always say."

The two girls rested propped up with pillows on the floor of DJ's bedroom, frequently dipping into a giant bowl of popcorn. The item of the evening: plans.

"I know what we can do about Tony. If everyone ignores him and we all pretend he isn't around, pretty soon he'll quit the Academy. And then Hilary won't have a problem anymore." DJ rolled over to her belly, the better to reach the popcorn. "It's got to work." She stuffed a handful of popcorn into her mouth and licked her buttery fingers.

"But we can't tell Hilary." Amy sat up. "She'll be furious—Bridget too."

"I know, that's the hard part."

"How are we going to let all the others know without them finding out?"

"I'll take care of that."

"Now *that's* a scary solution." Amy ducked to escape the pillow DJ threw. "Let's go to bed—I'm beat."

"No way. Now we need to work on the major plan." DJ twisted her mouth from side to side. "The plan of all plans—to keep my mother from marrying Robert."

"You know how cruel that sounds?"

"You've got to be kidding. You should have seen the way Robert took over the other night. 'DJ, set the table. DJ, entertain the Double Bs. DJ . . .' You'da thought I was the nanny or something." DJ ignored the twinge of guilt she felt. Even she could recognize exaggeration.

"So . . . could be worse." Amy dug a hull out from between two teeth.

"Whose side are you on, anyway?"

Amy shrugged. "I like Robert. But more than that, I know you do, too. And it's obvious what your mother thinks. Who knows? It could be fun to have him for a dad."

DJ stared at her friend. Had Amy read her mind again? "It's a matter of principle."

"You talked to Gran?"

"Sure, I was there the other night, remember?" DJ tried to find a comfortable position. She smacked the pillows behind her into a new shape and then repeated the effort. But when she leaned back, something poked her.

"I mean about the wedding."

Ignoring Amy, DJ punched her pillows again. "You want something else to drink?"

Amy sloshed her can. "Nope." She got to her feet and picked up her sleeping bag. "How about we sleep out on the deck? Pretty soon it'll be too cold."

A few minutes later, stretched out in their sleeping bags on the lounges, they stared up at the black sky. A jet winked its way east. The sliver of moon hung above the tallest eucalyptus trees, as if tethered like a kite.

A dog barked. DJ recognized the Rottweiler from two doors down. From a distance came the muted roar of the freeway. The light from the master bathroom clicked off, leaving the house dark except for the lamp in the family room.

"We'd have to leave this house if Mom and Robert go through with it." The breeze carried DJ's soft voice.

"The house isn't the same anyway without Gran."

"Do you have to have an answer for everything?" While meant as a joke, DJ felt like slamming her fist on the redwood deck. "I don't *want* to move. I don't *want* a new father. I don't even care about the one I do have." Quiet for a minute. " 'Course I might if I knew my real dad, but I don't. And I most especially don't want . . ."

A cricket answered her, and a soft snuffle told her that Amy had fallen asleep.

I don't know what I want anymore. DJ turned over and replayed her pillow-thumping routine. It didn't help any more now than it had earlier. What was she going to do?

The next morning, both girls hurried through cleaning their required stalls and grooming at the Academy. Amy and her family were going into San Francisco, and DJ was going with Joe and Gran to Redding to look at a couple of cutting horses for Joe. With Tony nowhere in sight, they didn't have to worry about putting their plan into action.

Saturday mornings were usually spent riding and practicing. Sometimes DJ taught a class. This Saturday, the plan added an extra task. Every time DJ saw one of the other student workers, she pulled that person aside and explained the plan. "Don't talk to Tony Andrada" became the password of the day. DJ told each person to pass it on but to make sure Tony, Hilary, and Bridget didn't hear about it. By the time she'd worked both Major and Patches, the hands on her wristwatch were already close to eleven.

Amy had finished and gone home an hour earlier.

DJ rode into Gran and Joe's drive just as they were loading things into his green Ford Explorer.

"You're just in time." Gran turned from packing the fishing tackle box that held all her paints.

"I thought we were going to look for horses." DJ dropped a kiss on her grandmother's rose-scented cheek.

"You're dropping me off at the Viano Winery so I can paint, then picking me up on the way back." Gran gave DJ a quick one-arm hug. "I haven't gotten to do a landscape for a long time, and the hills covered with grape vines are so beautiful this time of year."

"You're busy 'cause you keep getting more contracts for books." DJ rubbed her stomach. "Anything to eat? I'm starved."

"So what's new?" Joe came out of the house with a cooler and picnic basket in hand. "I brought plenty so you can start munching immediately if you need to."

"Thanks. How come you already know me so well?"

"I raised three kids, that's why." Joe set the food boxes on the floor. "And teenagers, whether male or female, are always hungry. It's a universal law."

"You should know, Mr. Policeman." DJ leaned in and flipped open the cooler to extract a soda and an apple.

"Mr. Ex-policeman, you mean." He held the front door open so Gran could climb into the Explorer. "Last call for anything you've forgotten."

As soon as they were on the road, DJ dug a bologna and cheese sandwich out of the cooler and a bag of chips from the basket. "Anyone else want anything?" she asked just before sinking her teeth into the sandwich. Gran had even baked bread.

"No, thanks."

After they dropped Gran off to paint, DJ moved to the front seat and propped her knees on the dash. "I think you should buy Gran a horse, too."

"I offered, and she said no thank you but we could buy one for the other grandkids if I liked."

"That's like Gran. I know she would love riding up in Briones. She could find some neat places to paint. You know, if you want to ride Major up there, I can always take Megs. She's feeling left out since I got Major." Megs belonged to Bridget and had been retired from showing.

"We'll see. I might have a horse of my own after today."

But that was not to be. DJ took an instant dislike to the first horse they looked at. "I don't care if his bloodlines go clear back to Spain, his back legs are bad. As he gets older, they'll just get worse." The Bridgetlike comments rolled off DJ's tongue.

Joe gave her a smile. "I saw that, too, but he is well trained."

"You can train one just as well."

The second horse required more deliberation. Joe rode the chestnut gelding around the ring, putting it through what paces it had. The ad had stated the horse was green broke, and it wasn't kidding.

"He'll grow some." The owner leaned on the board fence beside DJ. "His sire has taken awards up and down the coast. We'll be entering him in Nationals next year. And his dam has produced two Nationals winners already."

DJ listened to his sales pitch and watched Joe on the horse. "He'll take a lot of training." The gelding was refusing to switch leads or stand still.

"True, but he hasn't learned any bad habits, either. I broke him myself, so I know he's a willing learner."

Joe rode the horse up to the fence. "What do you think, DJ? He's fairly easy gaited. You ride him and see what you think."

DJ adjusted the stirrups on the Western saddle and swung aboard. The horse reminded her of Patches, all go and no brains. What would Bridget say? The bloodlines were good, the confirmation okay—near as she could tell—

and the price wasn't too bad for a three-year-old registered Quarter Horse.

Joe thanked the man and promised they'd get back to him in a day or so. They discussed the pros and cons of the horse on the way back to pick up Gran, but still had reached no decision by the time they got home.

"Well, my darlings, I say if you have to talk about that horse this much, then he isn't the one to buy. When you see the right one, I think you'll know right away." Gran carefully lifted her easel out of the car so she wouldn't smear the still-wet oil paints.

"Sort of love at first sight, you mean?" Joe handed DJ the cooler and hamper while he retrieved the remainder of their gear.

"Y'all could call it that."

"But, Gran, there are so many things to consider."

"You'll see."

DJ and Joe swapped there-she-goes-again looks.

But DJ had learned through the years that when Gran gave her opinions, they were usually right. "Have you been praying for a horse for Joe?"

"Of course, child. Why wouldn't I?" Gran stopped with one foot on the bottom step. "There is nothing so small that God doesn't want us to talk it over with Him. Why, I even talk to Him about what to serve for dinner."

DJ followed her into the house. The delicious smells of garlic and tomato sauce greeted them.

"And what did He say today?" DJ sniffed appreciatively.

"Lasagna. The salad's all tossed, and the garlic bread's ready for the oven." Gran glanced at her watch. "Lindy and Robert will be here with the boys any minute now. Thank goodness for ovens with timers."

DJ groaned. "Why didn't anyone tell me they were coming?"

"Why, what difference does it make?" Gran looked at

her as if she'd grown horns or something.

"I didn't bring clean clothes. You know how she hates it when I smell like horse."

"Do you want me to take you home to change?" Joe dropped a kiss on the back of Gran's neck as he walked by.

"You needn't worry—I washed the jeans and shirt you left here last time you spent the night." Gran gave DJ a gentle shove toward the bedroom. "You can shower, too, if it would make you feel better."

"There's the car. I'll keep the Double Bs busy until you're ready." Joe winked at DJ. "They think grandpas are *almost* as good as a big sister." He ducked away from her fake punch.

"I'll just ignore them all and hide out in here," DJ muttered to the pounding water. But she knew that wouldn't work. Her stomach was growling in anticipation of the lasagna. Besides, she knew her mother would threaten general destruction if she tried such a thing. Anything too obnoxious, and she might be grounded again. Now *that* was a fate worse than death. Last time—actually the one and only time it had ever happened to her—had nearly done her in.

DJ turned off the shower and dressed quickly. The laughter from the other room beckoned almost as persuasively as the lasagna and garlic bread.

The Double Bs' giggles were more catching than poison oak.

DJ forced her lips to stay in a straight line at their first elephant joke. Baby stuff.

She couldn't remember the answer to the second. It had been a long time since she'd heard an elephant joke.

But she knew the answer to the third. When Robert paused for someone to answer, she couldn't resist. "Footprints in the Jell-O."

"Huh?" The B on her right looked up at her.

"You can tell an elephant's been in the refrigerator by the footprints in the Jell-O." Left B started to giggle, then right B got the joke and the giggles turned to hoots. Very contagious.

DJ glanced up to see Robert smiling at her. Gran and Joe were chuckling with the boys. DJ sneaked a peek at her mother. Lindy had *never* appreciated stupid jokes. But growing up, DJ hadn't much minded because Gran had always been there to laugh with her.

When the giggles subsided somewhat, Robert asked, "How can you tell if there's an elephant in a cherry tree?"

"How?"

DJ had to bite her tongue. The silly answers were coming back to her.

Oh, fiddle. DJ leaned to her right and whispered in that B's ear. "Because elephants always wear red tennies."

"'Cause elephants gots red pennies."

DJ rolled her eyes. She tried again. "Tennies, B, *tennies*."

"'Cause the tree gots tennies."

The other B laughed so hard he fell off his chair.

"You okay?" DJ leaned down and helped him up.

"Tennies in the tree! Elephants wear red tennies in the cherry tree so we can see 'em." He looked up at her to make sure he had gotten it right.

In shifting from one twin to the other, DJ caught a glimpse of her mother's face. Lindy wore a half smile, the polite kind, the kind that DJ knew meant her mother was only half there. The rest of her was probably selling more guns to the police departments or planning her thesis.

What she wasn't doing was having fun.

"Can I be excused?" DJ pushed her chair back from the table. "Come on, guys. I'll race you to the road and back."

DJ hoped the breeze in her hair and on her face would blow away the anger she felt toward her mother right now.

Why couldn't she laugh at a little joke? Just to be part of the group. It wasn't as if her mother didn't know how. *Maybe she didn't get the joke. Or maybe she's a snob.* The thoughts raced through DJ's mind as her feet pounded the gravel.

Careful to keep even with the running boys, she reached down for their hands, and together the three sprinted the last few yards.

"I won."

"No, me!"

"Hey, guys, we all won." That was the way it was supposed to be, wasn't it? Everyone winning?

DJ tickled one twin and then the other. "Race you back to the house." They darted off and she followed, this time letting them win by a jump or two.

Before falling asleep that night, DJ looked up at the poster of the Olympic rider and horse clearing the jump and prayed, "God, I really need a way to stop my mom and Robert from getting married. A plan with a capital *P*." She tacked another line on to her prayer to cover all the bases. "And, God, please help my mother to laugh. She wouldn't even smile at the elephant jokes."

Did God really have a plan in all this?

7

TWO WEEKS PASSED AND STILL DJ HAD NO PLAN. Worse yet, Tony Andrada continued making life at the Academy miserable for all of them. DJ felt as though something in her life wasn't working—like everything. On top of all that, she'd been notified that she had received only an honorable mention in the art contest.

"What's so great about an honorable mention?" she sighed to Amy.

"Most people would be pumped about an honorable mention." Amy shook her head. "But not *my* friend. *My* friend likes only blue ribbons."

"No, I'd take a purple rosette, too." DJ licked the other side of her mocha almond fudge ice-cream cone. The two girls had bicycled down to the local shopping center for "some real food," as DJ called it. Her mother was on a low-fat kick again and had only rabbit food in the house. Or at least, that's what DJ called all the vegetables.

"Mom wants to lose weight, so I get to starve." DJ took a bite of her sugar cone and closed her eyes in bliss. "Why don't we go to the exhibit and see what kind of illustration took grand prize? I thought my horse was pretty good, and even Gran said I'd done well. You know what a perfectionist she is about artwork."

"Okay, but how are we going to get there?"

"Bus. I could ask Gran, though. Maybe she'd like to see it, too—of course, she would, my picture's hanging there," DJ thought aloud.

"What about your mom?"

"Ha! You know she's been to only one—no, make that two—of my horse shows since I began showing. What kind of a mother is she, anyway?"

"A busy one." Amy finished her cone and tossed the wrapper into the trash.

"Your father goes to every show, and your mom makes most of them." DJ leveled a look at her friend that dared her to get out of this one.

"I know. But my mom says it's easier to make it to things like that when you're a stay-at-home mother."

"Yeah, *you* never have to come home to an empty house."

"Sometimes I'd like to." Amy shoved up the kickstand on her bike.

"Feel free to visit mine any day."

"Mom won't let me—there's no adult there." Amy tipped her head and licked her lips.

DJ knew the gesture meant Amy was trying to keep from laughing.

"See what I mean?"

"You know what it's like at our house. You have to shout to make yourself heard. With four kids, I have to lock the bathroom door for some privacy—then John always has to go."

DJ often dreamed of becoming a member of the Yamamoto clan. Having brothers and sisters around had always sounded neat.

Until now. Now brothers and sisters meant the Double Bs.

"You're lucky to have an older brother."

"You want him, you can have him." Amy slung her leg over the bicycle. "You ready? I have to clean my room. With the show next weekend, I promised I'd do it today."

DJ glanced up at the fading light. "You better hurry, the day's about gone."

"I know. You could come help me."

DJ thought of the quiet house that awaited her. Lindy was off doing research to help her decide on a thesis topic. The note she'd left said she'd be home by dinner. She didn't mention who was cooking it or eating it.

"Sorry, but I better not. I think I'm supposed to be at home or Gran's."

"You think?" The two pedaled side by side up the residential street.

"Well, you know . . . Mom and I haven't been communicating much lately, at least not speaking. She writes me notes or leaves messages on the machine. Easier that way."

"Is she coming to the horse show?"

"Dream on. It's no big deal. When she is there, my butterflies invite all their friends in and have a party—at my stomach's expense." DJ kept pedaling and stretched her arms above her head. "Gran and Joe will be there, and they're the ones who count."

"You going to church with them in the morning?"

"Yep."

"You could ride with us if you want."

DJ sometimes wished her mother would come along, too, but Lindy used Sunday mornings to study. She said Gran could take care of the praying and churchgoing for their family. Lindy didn't want to be bothered with it.

The message light blinked on the machine. "DJ, I'm at Robert's. I'll be home late. Robert would like us all to go to church together tomorrow, so tell Gran you'll be going with us."

"With us where? I don't want to go to some strange church in the city. I like our church." DJ slammed the replay button. The message sounded no better the second time.

I think I'll go sleep with Major, that way I won't have to go with anyone. What about my Sunday school class?

Doesn't my mother ever think of anyone but herself? Since when does she go to church? Just because Robert asked her? DJ fussed and fumed until she climbed into bed.

"Great, she didn't even mention what time we're leaving." DJ debated going downstairs and leaving a message on the machine herself. But instead she set her alarm for an early wake-up. She had to feed Major no matter what.

It wasn't hard to pull off the silent act the next morning. By the time she returned from the Academy, Lindy was in a fit. DJ had barely ten minutes to get ready.

"And don't you dare make us late," Lindy yelled above the sound of the shower.

DJ soaped and rinsed as quickly as if she were a four-handed alien. There wasn't time to wash her hair; she'd have to braid it in the car. Half dry, she dashed into her bedroom and into her underwear. Putting on a bra with a wet back wasn't easy, but the real problem hit when she opened her closet: no dress pants. She'd forgotten to put her laundry in the dryer again.

"Mom, I'm gonna have to wear jeans," she called, hunching her shoulders against the tirade she knew was coming, at the same time buttoning a teal blouse and adding a vest.

"Why can't you at least dress up for church?" Lindy stopped in the doorway. "Where are all your good pants?"

"In the washing machine."

"I can tell your chores are getting to be too much for you. You'll just have to—"

The doorbell rang.

"We'll discuss this later." In her ivory silk suit and matching hat and shoes, Lindy looked as if she'd just stepped out of a Macy's display window.

DJ grumbled under her breath, grabbed her suede shoes, and pounded down the hall. She snagged a brush and a hair band from the bathroom before leaping down the stairs. So she didn't have dress pants on—she looked pretty good as far as she could tell. Jeans were always in style.

But they certainly weren't her mother's idea of a fashion statement.

The day went downhill from there. While the boys squirmed only a little during the opening prayer, they both let out soft whoops of joy when it came time for the children's sermon and then children's church.

Although the San Francisco church had beautiful stained-glass windows and a neat folk choir, DJ missed her Sunday school class.

At the restaurant where they went for brunch, Bobby—or was it Billy?—spilled his orange juice. While Lindy said it didn't matter, the stain showed up bright orange on her silk skirt. DJ kept herself from laughing only through sheer strength of will.

As Robert scolded the culprit, DJ dropped her fork. Bending to retrieve it, she bumped her plate—which bumped her water goblet. The goblet tipped, and water spread across the tablecloth. For the second time that morning, Robert called the waiter for assistance.

"I'm sorry." She didn't dare look at her mother. The vibes coming across the table told her enough.

"Accidents will happen." Robert tried to smooth things over.

Bobby sniffed on the chair beside DJ. Billy acted as though he'd been scolded, too.

As DJ had thought, silence was the best defense, or offense, as the case may be—in this case, anyway.

Telling Amy about it the next day, DJ couldn't help but laugh. "My mother does *not* like scenes in restaurants or church or anywhere."

"Did you drop your fork on purpose?"

"Gimme a break. Even I wouldn't dare do something like that."

"Did you ask her about the jumping clinic at Wild Horse Valley?"

"Fiddle. How could I forget something like that?" DJ shook her head. "I'm losing it, I tell you." They hopped off their bikes as they arrived at the Academy. "I'll ask tonight. We're having dinner at Gran's."

"Mrs. Johnson wants you to show Patches next weekend," Bridget informed DJ when she and Amy stopped in her office to say hello. "I said it was up to you."

"You think he's ready?" DJ picked at her fingernail.

"It would be good experience for both of you."

"Sure then. Why not?"

"Joe found his cutting horse yet?" Bridget asked.

DJ shook her head.

"I got a call from a friend who has been keeping an eye out for one. I missed Joe when he was here today taking care of Major. I will give him a call."

DJ flashed Amy a grin. "He'll be thrilled. Where is it?"

"Sacramento." Bridget shooed them out the door. "You two have work to do."

Tony was already in the ring practicing when they walked past. The two girls stopped for a moment to watch. The boy and horse moved as if they were welded together.

DJ felt a surge of envy. Tony and his horse were already at level two in dressage, and she had barely begun. The horse floated around the ring, each leg extended and then placed with precision. Tony didn't seem to move a muscle.

"It's just not fair," DJ muttered, turning to the barns. "Tony is such an excellent rider, and yet he's meaner than a—"

"Rabid skunk?"

"Yeah, and twice as smelly." DJ picked up her grooming bucket and headed for Patches' stall. She had plenty of work to do if they were going to show.

"Major, you must be the most willing horse in the world," DJ said later after putting the big bay through his paces. She leaned forward and rested her cheek on his mane, wrapping both arms around his neck. "You are so easy to love."

"Now that's as nice a picture as I have yet to see. Wish I had a camera so Melanie could paint you."

"Hi, Joe." DJ straightened to see her grandfather leaning against the aluminum fencing of the jumping arena. "You hear the news?"

"Sure enough. Think we could go over there and look at him this evening?"

In her mind, DJ flashed to her backpack at home. All she really had to do tonight was read a chapter for history, and she could do that in the car. "Sure." Then her excitement drooped. "I should ask Mom first. I thought we were having dinner at your house."

"That was the plan. Lindy called and asked if we could put dinner off till tomorrow. Something came up at work she had to deal with right away."

On one hand DJ thought, *Figures, her work always comes before the rest of us,* and on the other, she was thrilled to have the evening free. "Why don't you ask her while I finish my lesson. Is Gran coming, too?"

"Yep. We'll stop for dinner after we see the horse." He held up one hand. "I know, I know—bring food, you'll be starved."

DJ grinned and blew him a kiss. "See ya."

Her lesson with Bridget was a challenge. Bridget claimed that if you learned the finer points of jumping right the first time, it saved hours of relearning. But sometimes the first time meant weeks of drilling and redrilling.

And DJ loved every minute of it. Neither she nor Major

resented the repetition. Jumping was jumping. Each moment they spent airborne, DJ felt like yelling for pure joy. One time around, she became aware of Joe watching from the sidelines, but she kept her focus on her hands, her feet, her seat, her posture, and Major. After each jump, she looked forward to the next—the height, the length, and the timing. At last, some things were becoming enough of a habit that she could concentrate on others.

"Very good." Bridget met her at the gate when the lesson was over. "You can be proud of your granddaughter, Joe. And your horse."

"Oh, I am. No doubt about it." Joe stroked Major's sweaty neck. "God gave me a gift here," he laid a hand on DJ's knee, "that I'll never be able to thank Him for enough. That was some ride, kid."

"Thanks, GJ." DJ wanted to hug her horse, her grandfather, and even the fence post. For the first time in a while, Bridget hadn't had to call her on concentration.

"By the way, DJ." Bridget looked up at the rider. "Is there something you would like to tell me about Tony Andrada?"

DJ swallowed. She cleared her throat. "Ah . . . no, not really." What was Bridget referring to? Had someone blabbed about the silent treatment? "Why?"

"Oh, a little bird told me about something going on in the barns, and I have a feeling the hand of DJ Randall is all over it."

DJ swallowed again. She couldn't lie. *Please, Bridget, don't ask me any more. Especially not now with Joe here.*

"I will leave it for now, but make sure no one gets hurt."

DJ nodded.

"What was that all about?" Joe asked after Bridget left for her office.

"Tell you later." DJ nudged Major forward. "If we're going to Sacramento, we better get moving."

Joe brought up the subject of Tony once they were on the road to Sacramento. DJ had already put away a soda, six chocolate chip cookies, and an apple.

She tossed the core into the garbage and wrinkled her nose, hoping that would help her think better. "Well, you've heard me say what a creep Tony Andrada is."

"I gathered that he wasn't your favorite student worker."

"With good reason. He called Hilary a . . . ni—"

"DJ." Gran's gentle reminder made DJ stop midword.

"Well, that's not the worst thing he's called her, either. Is everyone from the South like him?"

"Darlin', I'm from the South."

"I know, that's why I'm asking." DJ thought about what she'd said. "But I don't mean you, of course. Just boys. Come on, Gran, you know what I mean."

"I do. And to answer your question, there are some people in the South—and other places, mind you—who think people with dark skin are of less value. It's that old slaveholder mentality. Sometimes I wonder if discrimination will ever end." She shook her head and turned to look at DJ. "But, darlin', I know you don't feel that way, and if more young people can grow up colorblind like you, our world will eventually become a better place."

"In the meantime, what have you cooked up?" Leave it to Joe to bring the subject back to DJ.

"Well, Amy and I have a plan to deal with Tony."

Gran groaned. "Heaven help us."

"Gr-a-n!"

"You have to admit some of your *plans* haven't worked out quite like you hoped." Gran's smile let DJ know she was teasing.

"I know, but this time . . . this time it *has* to work or Hilary will move her horse to another stable. That'll mess up her whole life."

"And your plan?"

"To ignore Tony. No one's supposed to talk to Tony. We pretend he isn't even there."

"And Hilary?"

"She doesn't know anything about it." DJ took a bite of the cuticle on her right pinkie as she waited out the silence in the front seat.

"So, how is it working?"

"Don't know. I haven't talked to Hilary lately, and the only time I see Tony is in the ring. Since he goes to a private school, his hours are different from mine." DJ clenched her hands in her lap. Why did she always want to chew her fingernails when she was uptight? She leaned her arms on the back of the front seat. "And you know what? *Amy* thinks he's cute!"

"So?"

"So how can anyone be cute when he talks like Tony?"

Gran chuckled. "That's one of the many things I love about you, darlin'. You look to the inside of a person, not just the outside."

"You know, your plan does have a sound basis." Joe caught DJ's eye in the rearview mirror.

"Really?"

"Sure. Ignoring bad behavior is a good way to make someone change. But to make the program really effective, you have to go one step further."

DJ unbuckled her seat belt so she could lean on the front seat without cutting off her circulation. "I hear you."

"You have to compliment him for doing the right thing."

"Right. The dinosaurs will return before I catch Tony doing something good."

Joe smiled at her. "I'm sure if you try, you'll find a way. And you better explain this addition to your plan to the others."

DJ thought about phrases like *a snowball's chance in that hot place reserved for people like Tony* and *when cows have wings*, but she kept them to herself. She did need to talk to the rest of the student workers, that was for sure.

She was still thinking about what Joe and Gran had said when they turned into an entrance arch with *Denison's Quarter Horses* painted in white across the top. Board-fenced fields lined the drive, and a barking border collie met them at the gate to the low, rambling house off the circular drive. A man donned his felt Western hat as he came down the steps toward them.

"You the fellow who wants to see my young cutting horse?" He extended a hand. "I'm Hank Denison."

After the introductions, he showed them where to park, and they followed him down to a shiny white barn. Horses blinked and nickered as he flicked on the light. "Rambling Ranger is right over here. I kept him in tonight when you said you were coming." He took a lead shank off a hook on the wall and led the way to the third stall on the left. A bright sorrel head with a perfect diamond between the eyes and another smaller one between flaring nostrils bobbed in greeting. The horse wuffled, his nostrils quivering as Denison snapped the lead shank onto the blue nylon halter.

"He's sixteen hands and three years old, as I told you on the phone, so he may grow a bit more. He'll fill out, anyway." As he spoke, Hank led the horse out of the stall. Both front feet had white socks nearly to the knees.

DJ fell in love. She looked up at Joe. His eyes were shining, too.

The horse moved with the natural grace of good confirmation and a style that came from excellent bloodlines. When Denison trotted, the gelding followed, his hooves clopping a steady rhythm on the hard-packed dirt.

"Let's go over to the covered arena, and I'll saddle him up for you. Now, remember he's only begun his training. I haven't worked him with cattle yet."

Joe and DJ walked around the horse, studying him from all angles as Denison saddled him. DJ couldn't find a thing wrong. How much was the man asking? She looked up at

Joe. The silly grin on his face said it all.

"I'll take him around a few times so you can watch him. Then you can try him out." Denison mounted as he spoke.

DJ and Joe watched without a word, sharing a glance of pure excitement. When the man returned to the rail and dismounted, he offered the reins to DJ.

"You better ride him first, GJ," DJ whispered.

Joe nodded. He stroked the horse's nose, then mounted when Denison handed him the reins.

DJ watched as her grandfather moved the horse through his gaits, reined him from side to side, and tried to get him to back up. Only then did Rambling Ranger balk for the first time.

"He don't like backing too much yet, but he learns quick." Denison rubbed the cleft in his chin with one finger.

DJ was doing her best to control her excitement. After all, when you bought something, you were supposed to be cool about it, not scream, "Yes! Yes! Yes!" like she wanted to.

"You want to ride, kid?" Joe stopped the horse in front of her.

"Sure." DJ changed places with her grandfather. She rode the horse around the ring, doing all the same things Joe had. "You're a dream come true, you know that?"

The horse twitched his ears, but he still didn't want to back up. DJ made him stand and then pulled firmly on the reins. Ranger shook his head but finally he backed—one step, then two. He sighed and kept on backing up until DJ let off the pressure. She patted his neck. "Good boy."

Rambling Ranger was perfect, but could Joe afford a horse like this?

8

"YOU BOUGHT HIM? Just like that?"

"He really did." Gran shook her head. "I knew I married a man who could make split-second decisions, and now I've seen him in action." Gran patted Joe's arm. "I'm glad for you, darlin'."

"Why don't we look for a horse for you while we're here?" Joe covered her hand with his. "You have no idea what you're missing when you can't ride up in Briones with us."

DJ watched several expressions flit across her grandmother's face before a slight dip of her chin indicated she disagreed.

"But, Gran, you've never ridden around here. Have you ever ridden at all?" DJ asked.

"When I was younger." Gran reached up to stroke the gelding's nose. "I'm just glad you two can have your dreams of showing. I'll come along to cheer you on."

DJ and Joe swapped looks. They were going to have to work on this. If they were to become a horse family, Gran would have to join in.

"So, when can you deliver him?" Joe turned to Denison and took out his checkbook. "I need to have a barn built, but in the meantime I'll stable him at the Briones Riding Academy where my granddaughter works and rides. The owner, Bridget Sommersby, gave me your name."

"Day after tomorrow soon enough?" Denison led Rambling Ranger back to his stall and removed the tack.

"That'll be just fine."

DJ felt as though she'd been struck by lightning. Any time she'd wanted anything, there'd always been a big discussion, a plan to earn or save the money, and then usually a big "no" from her mother. Horses and horse things weren't high on Lindy's list of priorities, unlike school and fashionable clothing and—DJ cut off that line of thought as she rubbed down the horse's shoulder. Ranger sure was a beauty. He and Joe looked wonderful together.

She was still bubbling when she walked in the door at home and found Lindy and Robert looking through the photo albums DJ and Gran had spent so many hours putting together.

"Mom, you won't believe it. GJ bought his horse!" She grinned at Robert, who sat beside her mother. "You got some dad there. Wait till you see him—the horse I mean. His name is Rambling Ranger, but we're gonna call him Ranger." DJ didn't take time to breathe.

"Sounds like my dad all right." Robert stretched his hands above his head. "I better get going. Full day ahead."

"Hey, Mom, I forgot to ask. There's a jumping clinic coming up at Wild Horse Ranch in Napa, and Bridget thinks it would be good for me and Major to go. What do you think, can I?"

"Can you afford it?" Lindy let Robert pull her up from the sofa. She smiled up at him with one of those gooey looks DJ was coming to expect from the two of them.

"Well, I'm trying to save for a Crosby—that's a good make of jumping saddle. I was kind of hoping maybe you could swing this." DJ clamped her bottom lip between her teeth.

"You know the rules." Lindy adjusted her slacks. "You can go only if you can afford the time and the money."

"How much is it?" Robert looked from mother to daughter.

When DJ told him the amount, he reached for his wallet. "Why don't you let me get this one?"

"No." One word from Lindy stopped him in the act.

He turned to her, surprise written across his handsome face. "But why?"

DJ bit her tongue to keep from telling him how she felt. *Because my mother always has money for her things, but mine don't count. Get it?*

"Because *I* can't afford it, and I'm raising my daughter to be a responsible person who earns her own way."

Robert started to say something and stopped.

"DJ understands."

Yeah, right! Sure I understand. DJ felt like yelling. She had no time now to earn extra money. Other kids baby-sat. She and Amy had given pony parties for kids' birthdays during the summer, but now her time was all taken up with school, the Academy, and home chores. Her mother was the one who didn't understand.

Or maybe she doesn't care. The thought shocked DJ into continued silence.

"Well, why don't you let this be my gift to DJ?"

DJ felt a stirring of hope.

"That's very nice of you, but no thank you. DJ, don't you have homework to finish?"

"No, I'm done." DJ knew that had been the signal for her to leave the room, but instead she dug in her heels. She still might have a chance if she played it right.

DJ sneaked a peek at Robert. His smile had disappeared along with his wallet. Questions pounded in her head. What was wrong with Robert's giving her a present? Lindy had already accepted several gifts for herself: a bracelet, a designer scarf, and a program for her computer. So why was it okay for her mother to get presents, but not her? A hangnail on DJ's right thumb itched to be chewed off. She dug at it with her finger.

"Say good-night, DJ."

DJ did as she was told, barely holding back from stomping up the stairs.

This was one of those nights when she wished with all her might that Gran was still living in the same house. Gran would be able to explain her mother's actions to her—they made no sense at all to DJ. She knew she could call Gran and talk about it, but somehow the phone wasn't the same as sitting at Gran's feet. She *needed* Gran's gentle hands on her hair and the smell of roses and Gran saying, "Well now, darlin', I think we should pray about this and see what God has to say about it."

DJ tried. "Heavenly Father, I don't understand my mother at all. Sometimes I don't even like her." She stopped. She shouldn't say such things even though she thought them a lot. But her Sunday school teacher had said God knew people's thoughts even before they spoke them.

DJ shuddered. Some of her thoughts sure weren't the kind she wanted God listening in on.

What was the Bible verse Gran had given her recently? She wrinkled her forehead, hoping that would make her remember. Something about God answering our prayers. She'd have to ask Gran because DJ sure needed some answers right now. She moved on to all the "blesses," including Robert and the Double Bs. "And, God, thank you for finding Grandpa Joe such a neat horse. Amen."

How on earth was she going to earn the money for the clinic?

Both DJ and Amy were out of breath when they spun into the academy parking area the next afternoon. They spied Joe's Explorer immediately.

"Is he here yet?" DJ pelted into Bridget's office. "Where's his stall?"

"Should I ask who 'he' is?" Bridget looked up from her

charting with a smile. She raised a hand to cut off DJ's questions. "Outside stall, next to Major. I figured since Joe feeds both of them in the morning, we should make it as easy as possible."

"What do you think of him? Didn't we do great?"

"He is everything Denison said he was. Now Joe has to decide if he will train Ranger himself or hire a trainer." Bridget waved the girls toward the door. "Go on before you wear a hole in the floor."

The girls dashed across the lot and jogged down the sandy barn aisle. Horses nickered on either side, and one slammed a hoof against the wall with a squeal.

When they found them, Joe had one of Ranger's hooves propped on his knees to pick out any compacted manure and dirt. The crosstied sorrel stood quietly, showing that he'd been trained in being handled.

"He's beautiful, Joe." Amy and DJ stopped at the stall opening.

Joe stood up, and stroking the gelding as he walked, joined the two girls.

"I'm pretty pleased myself." He rubbed up behind Ranger's ears and down his neck. "He and I are going to get along just fine, aren't we, boy?" Ranger reached his nose out to sniff the girls, who stood still for his inspection. Ears forward, he sniffed at DJ's extended hand. She turned it over to palm a horse cookie for him.

"Now you've made a friend." Joe continued to stroke the horse as he talked. "Denison said Ranger has a weakness for sugar lumps, but cookies and carrots are definitely better, right, fella?" Ranger nosed DJ for another treat.

"Have you ridden him yet?" Amy asked.

"Nope, he arrived not more than an hour ago. I figured I'd let him get accustomed to the stable first and ride tomorrow morning when the arenas aren't taken up by you kids." He picked up a brush and stroked down the already gleaming shoulder.

Next to them, Major nickered and tossed his head.

"He's jealous." Joe nodded to his former horse. "I kept telling him you'd be by pretty soon, but he didn't believe me."

DJ switched her attentions to the bay. Major nosed the pocket where she always kept his treat. She dug out a cookie and let him munch. "See, that wasn't your treat I gave away. That young sprout may be getting all the attention right now, but that's because he's new."

"And pretty." Amy moved to Major's side and stroked his dark neck.

Major whiskered DJ's cheek and made her giggle.

"You just wait a bit, and I'll be back to get you." DJ gave her horse one last ear rub and stepped back. "Got work to do. Behave now." The horse tossed his head and nodded as if he understood everything she said. "See ya, GJ."

"You going to braid his mane and tail for the show?" Amy asked.

"No, not for the training show. But for the one in December I will. Just think, that will be our first big show. Mine and Major's, I mean."

"You think Joe will enter that one?"

"He could, in halter class at least. Even halter showing would give Ranger a feel for the crowds and activity."

They stopped in the door of the barn when they heard an angry voice coming from the south side stalls.

"I don't have to listen to you, you stupid jigaboo! My dad is going to talk to Bridget and get me assigned to someone with some real horse sense. Everyone knows niggers don't have no sense a'tall."

"Listen here, Tony, I have my assignments, and I do them. You have been assigned to me, and that places me in charge. Now get back there and redo that stall. We don't allow people to pitch fresh shavings on top of dirty ones."

"If you're so all-fired worried about doing things right, *you* do it."

DJ and Amy peeked around the corner just in time to

see Tony shove the handle of the manure fork at Hilary. She wasn't prepared, and it knocked her on the shoulder before she could stop it.

"I have better things to do." Tony made a rude gesture and strode down the aisle to where his horse stood looking over the gate of its stall.

DJ debated. Should they go to Hilary, or was it better to let her friend handle this alone? In the end, she signaled Amy, and they headed back to their side of the barn.

"Well, that sure shows our plan isn't working." DJ slammed her hand against the wall. "How can we help Hilary?"

"Short of dumping a ton of hay on that . . . that creep. Why'd he ever choose to come here anyway?"

"Because Bridget is such a good teacher, that's why." DJ rubbed the palm of her hand to remove the sting of slapping it on the wood. "Why didn't Hilary shove the handle right back at him? I would have. I'd have picked it up and bashed him over the head with it. Nobody but nobody's ever gonna get away with calling *me* names like that. Should we tell Bridget?"

Amy shook her head. "I don't know."

"You know what? I talked about this with Gran and Joe, and Joe said just ignoring Tony wasn't enough. He said we need to *compliment* him when he does something right. Can you beat that?"

"Yeah, as if he's going to do something good. Get real." Amy picked up a grooming bucket. "I've got to get going, or I won't have time to work Josh. DJ, something's got to get better around here, or Hilary will leave—and I wouldn't blame her a bit."

By Friday, DJ's butterflies were in full flight. All she could think of was the show coming up the next day. Even though it was only a schooling show, this would be only the second time she showed Major, and she was going to enter Patches, too. All that plus coaching her three students and helping wherever Bridget needed her.

"Would you like to join us in class, DJ?" Her history teacher eyed her curiously over her glasses.

DJ could feel the heat begin at her collarbone and race up her face. "I . . . I'm sorry." If only she could slither down under her desk and out the door.

"Please join us on page ninety-three and read from the second paragraph."

"Yes, ma'am." DJ found the place and rose to her feet. She heard someone snicker behind her. Now even her ears burst into flame. Reading aloud forced her to keep her mind on the lesson.

"Thank you," the teacher said when DJ reached the end of the section. "Next?"

DJ sank into her desk. At least she hadn't been asked a question on top of the reading. How embarrassing! If Bridget caught her daydreaming like that, she'd have had to do extra stalls.

The barns were in a flurry that afternoon with everyone bathing the show horses, then grooming them till they could nearly see their faces in the shiny hides. With two horses to prepare, DJ felt as if her arms would drop off by the time she finished. The white blaze on Patches' face shone like new-fallen snow when the sun struck it.

"You know, if you could behave as well as you clean up, you'd have it made." She slapped his rump to keep him from leaning on her while she picked his hooves. "You know all kinds of tricks to make my life miserable, don't you?"

The gelding snorted and twitched his tail, catching some hairs in DJ's mouth. She spit them out and brushed others off her head. "Sometimes I wonder about you, and other times I *know* you're rotten clear through."

"I really should be helping you so I learn how to do all this," Mrs. Johnson said from her position at the gate.

DJ flinched. Here she'd been saying bad things about the horse, and the owner was standing right there. *Stupid horse, why didn't he warn me?* She finished with the hooves and came around to drop the pick into the bucket. "You could keep brushing him and comb out his mane and tail."

"Sure." The woman ducked under the gate, picked up both brushes, and set to work. "We bought a leather halter and lead shank for tomorrow. He looks real good in it. Maybe next time I can show him—in halter at least."

"Sure thing." DJ started to leave. "You'll be here in the morning for loading?"

"Wouldn't miss it." Mrs. Johnson stopped brushing. "DJ, I keep meaning to ask. How is Andrew coming with Bandit? Is he getting over the fear? We've been talking about it a little, but he doesn't say much."

"He's doing better. I guess sometimes it's hard to talk about."

"I would love to see him entered in a show, and I just know he would enjoy riding up in the hills."

"Yes, ma'am." DJ had her doubts about Andrew ever wanting to show, but she wouldn't voice them now. "See you in the morning."

DJ headed for Major's stall. Joe had washed the big gelding earlier in the day, so he only needed grooming. She glanced up to see clouds of red reflecting the setting sun. How could the time pass so quickly?

"You go check on your students—I've got everything under control here." Joe paused in his brushing of the big bay as DJ walked up. Major leaned against his ties, half asleep.

"Thanks." DJ turned and headed back to the barns. The girls should be in soaping their saddles by now. The three had all gotten soaked on the wash racks but helped each other so all the horses were clean and blanketed. They reminded DJ of her and Amy back when they were younger, all excitement and giggles.

"My arm's gonna fall off," Krissie groaned when she saw DJ. "This saddle is so big."

"Not really. It just seems that way when it's soaped up." DJ checked the carved designs on the skirts. "You better get the soap cleaned out of here. It'll show up white in the daylight."

Krissie groaned again. "I'd rather wash my horse any day."

Angie looked up from her bridle. "DJ, do you feel sick the night before a show?"

DJ nodded. "I got yelled at in school today because I was thinking about the show instead of history."

The three girls giggled. "Did you get detention?"

"No way. I wasn't *that* bad." DJ inspected the work of all three. "Looks pretty good. You need to be here by 6:30 A.M. to load your horses." More groans. "Sorry, but that's part of showmanship. And make sure all your clothes are ready tonight, too." It felt like a century since DJ had started showing, but it had only been three years. "Shine your boots, and—"

"Get plenty of sleep!" The three shouted in unison.

DJ tapped Krissie on the head. "Smart mouths. Any questions?" When they shook their heads, she glanced over at the cars where their mothers waited. "Good, then you better hustle. See you in the morning."

DJ headed back toward Major's stall. Tony Andrada appeared in the side aisle.

"Hi, DJ."

DJ looked the other way and kept walking.

9

"STUCK-UP!"

The name-calling hurt, but DJ kept right on going. No way would she say anything to Tony—not after the way he had treated Hilary. No matter what Joe said. Besides, DJ sure hadn't seen him doing anything right. If only she could shut off the part of her that made her feel lousy when she was being less than honest. Tony hadn't been mean to her. He only had this thing against Hilary because she was black. Had he been mean to Maria, a girl with a Hispanic heritage? And what about Amy? She was a Japanese American.

She shut off the thoughts, said good-night to Major, and after snagging Amy from the tack room, headed home. Would her mother be home or out with Robert? She sure was spending a lot of time with him.

"You want to ride over to the show with us in the morning?" Amy asked when they reached her house. A discussion about Tony had kept them occupied all the way home. As usual, there were no solutions, only more problems.

"If your dad doesn't mind."

"That's a silly thing to say. Why would he mind?"

DJ shrugged. "Okay, see ya."

No car in the drive, no lights on—obviously no one was

home. Was that good or bad? DJ put her bike away, checked for messages—none—then wandered up to her room. Maybe her mother had left a note on the bed again. No such luck. The phone rang just as she was getting sandwich fixings out of the refrigerator.

After a greeting, Gran continued. "Lindy phoned to say that Robert called her and asked if the two of you would take care of the twins for the weekend. Robert was called out of town unexpectedly, and the boys' nanny already had plans. Lindy's gone into the city to pick them up."

"But I have the show tomorrow."

"She knows that. I'll help tomorrow if needed."

"I thought you and Joe would be at the show, too."

"We will. Maybe we'll bring the boys along with your mother. We'll work something out. I said the boys could come here, but Lindy thought this might be a good idea. This way, you can see how you all do together."

DJ felt a shudder start at her toes and reach her ears before blowing out the top of her head. Robert wouldn't be there to calm them down. And her mother's patience level lately had been nonexistent. Some weekend this was going to be. After saying goodbye to Gran, she wished she'd asked to come spend the night there. At least it would be quiet.

She ate, then wandered up to Gran's old room. Since the bedroom set had moved to Gran's new home, the room was empty. DJ got two sleeping bags down from the storage closet and two pillows from the linen closet. After spreading them out on the floor, she tried deciding what would help the boys feel at home. A radio? No, too old. Stuffed animals? Sure. She took a couple of bears and a pony off the shelf in her room and set them on the sleeping bags.

In spite of her best intentions, the boys ended up on the floor in DJ's room.

"Okay, knock it off. I have to get up early."

"Us too. We help you."

DJ groaned at the thought. She hung over the side of her bed to watch the two boys, still bright-eyed and wired. "Do you two ever wind down?"

They shook their heads as if strung together.

"Well, you better now. No more giggling, no more talking, and don't snore."

At that, the giggles erupted again. DJ had used her sternest voice, but making them laugh made her feel giggly, too. How could she resist?

"You said your prayers yet?" She watched them shake their heads again. How could they do things in such perfect sync? "Okay, who's first?"

"We say them together." Both boys folded their hands on their chests and closed their eyes. "Dear God, bless Daddy, and Mommy in heaven, Grandpa and new Grandma, DJ, our maybe new mom, and Bandit. Please give us a new family soon and a pony—two ponies. Amen." Their eyes popped open. "We always say bless DJ. Is that okay?"

"You bet, I need as many blessings as I can get. Good night, guys."

"Good night, DJ. We love you." Both voices sounded as one.

DJ turned out the light and flipped over on her back. If the twins were praying for Lindy to be their new mother and she was praying that the wedding wouldn't happen, which prayer would God answer?

She closed her eyes and pictured the jumps at the show. Bridget always said to picture what you were going to do in your mind first and always to imagine yourself doing it perfectly. Imagining was easy. In her mind, DJ had jumped the entire Olympic course many times. She'd jumped in a Grand Prix and at the Cow Palace, too. She'd made every jump with room to spare and basked in the thunderous applause.

Now if only her butterflies would go to sleep along with the rest of her.

"What's wrong, DJ?" Joe asked in the morning at the Academy.

"Too many things on my mind."

"I always find that when I get in a situation like that, prayer helps more than anything else."

"Yeah, well I prayed last night and this morning. The boys woke up when my alarm went off, and let me tell you, there was no way I could concentrate. They were so noisy! I left them watching cartoons after promising them Mom and Gran would bring them later. You suppose I had that many questions when I was little?"

Joe nodded. "From what Melanie remembers, yes. Come on, let's get this guy loaded." Ranger pawed the shavings in the next stall. "Sorry, fella, you have to stay home today."

DJ led Major out to the trailer and walked him right in. Josh and Amy followed, then Hilary with her horse. Next they loaded Tony's Thoroughbred and the other jumpers since the jumping events were always held first. Equitation classes came later, in the afternoon. As soon as the first load of horses departed, they started on the other students' horses.

Finally, Joe called the jumpers to ride with him. DJ cringed. Would Tony join them? Sure enough. And Joe waved the creep to the front seat.

DJ felt as if she'd been smacked with a two-by-four. What was the matter with GJ? She and Amy swapped looks and made a place for Hilary. With five kids, the Explorer was full.

When Hilary slammed the side door, Tony opened his.

Joe put a hand on the boy's arm. "You're riding with us." He spoke in his policeman's stern voice. Tony slammed the door and snapped his seat belt. He hugged the door as if he might be contaminated by the others.

Joe tried to make conversation, but all anyone answered was "yeah" or "no" or even a shake of the head.

DJ's butterflies invented new stunts.

They pulled into the showgrounds right behind the long trailer.

"You'd think he was afraid of catching something from us," DJ muttered when Tony bailed out before the truck had finished moving.

"Yeah, as if you could catch black skin," Hilary said in the same undertone.

"*We're* the ones who might catch something," Amy added. "And I sure don't want what he's got."

"Me neither."

By the time they had the rope strung between trees and the horses spaced out, the second trailer arrived, and with it, the younger students.

DJ decided that if she heard her name called one more time, she would freak.

"Concentrate, DJ." Bridget accurately picked up on DJ's panic. "I will take care of the young ones until you are finished showing. Besides, their parents are here to help. They must learn what to do, too."

DJ nodded. "Thanks." But even when Joe put a hand on her shoulder to stop her mad scurrying, she felt like yelling. What was the matter with her? She'd never been this uptight before, not even the first time she showed.

DJ changed into her tan stretch pants, white turtleneck, and black tailored jacket. She tied her stock, watching the material drape in the mirror. After dusting off her velvet-covered helmet, she left the RV used as a dressing room and headed back for the lineup.

Joe waited with Major, who was polished to a super sheen.

"You're looking good, kid." He gave her a leg up and left one hand on her knee. "Come on, let's see a smile. This isn't the Olympic finals, you know."

"I know." DJ let out a deep breath. "I keep telling myself to focus, then someone calls my name and I'm off again."

"Well, let's get over to the warm-up ring, and you'll be fine."

Hilary rode in front of them, and Tony fell in behind as they followed the trail around the ring to a separate area where riders were already warming up their horses. DJ settled in her saddle, straightened her back, and reminded herself to always look ahead. She smiled at Joe and signaled Major to walk forward.

After several turns around the ring at a two-point trot, she eased him over to the cavalletti, the bars laid out parallel on the ground. She kept Major going straight and bending smoothly in the turns. All the hours she'd worked on the basics seemed to be paying off. He moved better than any well-oiled machine, his gait smooth and collected.

DJ could feel herself become more in tune with the movements, aware of the horses around them yet blanking out the rest of the world. She made a visual check, her body over her pelvis instead of settled back in the saddle like she used to ride. Sure enough, there was a straight line from her elbows to Major's mouth. Heels down and looking straight ahead, she glanced down—right away, Major changed the beat. Back around again, over the cavalletti, one and two, relaxed and aware. She kept giving herself mental orders, sounding just like Bridget had for so many sessions.

When the announcer called for Hunter Seat, she joined the lineup at the gate. There were four entries from

Briones Riding Academy in a class of ten. DJ waited her turn, keeping her mind on the horse beneath her and the class ahead.

Until Tony walked his horse up beside her and hissed out the side of his mouth, "Nigger lover."

DJ felt her body tense as if she'd been struck. "Why, you . . . you . . ."

Tony touched his whip to his helmet and trotted into the ring.

"Next." The ring assistant waved her forward.

DJ now understood the meaning of the phrase "seeing red." A brilliant haze seemed to separate her from the rest of the world. She signaled Major into a trot but let him stumble as they entered the ring. The judge was staring right at her.

Concentrate! Come on, DJ, don't let him get to you. She swallowed and forced herself to look straight ahead, focusing on Major's ears and the direction they were going. All around the ring she gave herself instructions, but too many times she called herself names at the same time. When they placed sixth, she knew it was her own fault. Major could have done better—all by himself. Hilary took the first, and Tony the red.

DJ had to smile at the look on the boy's face. He didn't like being beaten, and he sure didn't like being beaten by Hilary. There was justice in the world after all.

"What happened?" Joe confronted her as soon as she exited the ring.

DJ wanted to tell him. After all, he'd invited the creep to sit in front on the way over. But tattling had never been her style. And she resolved she wouldn't start now. But she *would* get even. If only she could figure out how.

Calling herself names had become a habit halfway through the Hunter/Jumper class. She knew she was jumping ahead of Major, but she couldn't seem to stop. As soon as he left the ground, she knew she'd signaled him to jump too soon. Up and nearly over, and—the tick reverberated through her head. The last fence. She held her breath, but the pole didn't fall. She finished the circle to a round of applause, but in her head, the names continued.

"I don't deserve a horse like you when I mess up like this," she told Major as she left the ring.

"Self-talk is for building up, not tearing down." Bridget stopped to check on DJ with clipboard in hand. "Sometimes we learn by our mistakes. But good riders, even when they make mistakes, do not waste time calling themselves names. Let it go and learn from it. You will do better next time."

DJ nodded. It was good advice, but could she figure out how to take it? She and Major still had a chance to show in English equitation that afternoon.

She looked up when she heard someone call her name. Two matching pairs of arms waved wildly from the log seating off to the side. Gran and Lindy had the twins corralled between them. DJ waved back and rode off to the lineup. Now she had to answer to her students and remind them not to commit the same mistakes. Yuck!

"Tough luck, DJ." Angie turned from wiping her horse's face with a soft cloth. "I thought you had it."

"I wish." DJ remained on Major to watch the final round. Hilary jumped cleanly. She and her horse looked as though they were having a party out there. *How can she handle the pressure?* DJ thought. Tony and one other person had already completed perfect rounds.

The other rider ticked on the next round with the jumps raised two inches. DJ held her breath and let it out with a shout when Hilary made another perfect round. So did Tony. DJ swallowed a groan. The young girls around her didn't need to know about the problem between them, so she kept her thoughts to herself.

"He's so cute," Krissie whispered to Sam.

DJ shook her head. If only he were as nice as he was good-looking.

The poles went up again. DJ sent a prayer heavenward for her friend.

Hilary jumped first, another perfect round.

"This is your day, buddy, keep it up." DJ and Amy stood shoulder to shoulder with Major on the outside, head drooping over DJ's shoulder so she would scratch his cheek.

Only a nicker broke the silence as Tony entered the ring. His horse seemed to fly over the jumps. The oxer, a double, triple uneven poles, crossed poles and a double oxer, and the final, a square oxer. A hind foot rang on the pole. The pole wobbled but remained in place.

The crowd groaned.

"And the winner of our Hunter/Jumper class today is Hilary Jones on her horse, Prince. Hilary is from the Briones Riding Academy. Come on over here, young lady, and accept this well-earned blue ribbon and a coupon for a sack of horse chow from the Concord Feed and Seed Company."

The arena assistant gave out the ribbons while the announcer continued. "We'll take a few minutes to clear the arena, then start the equitation classes. Let's give Hilary Jones and Tony Andrada, our second-place winner and also from Briones, a well-deserved hand."

"He's not a happy camper," Amy said with a shake of her head.

"You suppose that's his dad?" DJ looked over at the man talking with Tony just outside the ring entrance.

"Got me. I haven't seen him around the barns. Tony's mom picks him up."

DJ turned at familiar shouts from the Double Bs. Joe had one on each hand pulling him along. He stopped them before they could run into the horses. DJ turned Major and walked back to them so they could pet the horse.

"I wanted you to win. How come you hit the pole? Don't you like blue ribbons best? Major's the best horse, isn't he? I was scared you was gonna fall off. Can I ride now?"

DJ looked up to see a grin on Joe's face. "Kinda make you tired, don't they?"

She switched her attention back to the matched pair, who were dancing in place. "How can I answer anything when you don't give me a chance?" She looked back at Joe. "Put them up on Major, and I'll walk them around. Major's tired of standing still anyway." She wiped the smile off her face and gave orders once they were aboard. "Now, no yelling or banging your legs. You have to sit still. Grandpa Joe will walk beside you so you won't fall."

"We wasn't gonna fall off." They looked at her as if she'd said a nasty word.

"No, of course not. Now hang on. Front B, grab the mane, B in back, the saddle cantle." She pointed to the places as she spoke. Life would be a lot easier if she could tell them apart well enough to call them by name.

When they returned, it was time to help her students and get Patches ready for the Halter class. Mrs. Johnson had been grooming him till he gleamed. DJ was wishing she had entered him in the Walk/Jog class, too—anything to give him experience.

The twins had gotten restless, so Lindy took them home after DJ placed third in equitation for fourteen-and-under riders. She didn't feel too badly about the results—she and Major still had a lot of work to do on form and pacing.

"You could have brought Ranger for the Halter class," DJ told Joe as she snapped the lead into Patch's show halter.

"I know, but I'd rather get to know him better first. I'll

watch you now, and then you can coach me," Joe responded.

"That goes for me, too." Mrs. Johnson fell into step beside them as they walked the path around the arena. "This is so much more fun than riding up into the hills. You think I could show Patches?"

"Why not? Halter class is a good place to start, then Walk/Jog. These training shows make it really easy to begin."

"Not like the big one after Thanksgiving, huh?"

DJ felt a flurry of butterfly wings in her stomach. She *had* to do better at that show, and the competition was tougher there.

Patches loved the show-ring. He strutted as though he'd been showing for years.

"You big show-off," DJ whispered as the judge gave the flashy gelding the blue ribbon. "Now if you only minded this well when you were under saddle."

By the end of the day, DJ felt as if she'd been run over by a six-horse hitch—with each hoof hitting her twice. Besides that, her belly felt like it hadn't been fed in a week.

She hit the front door wanting nothing more than food and bed.

Instead, she had two tornadoes wrapped around her legs before she could close the door.

"We been waiting for you. Grandma baked cookies. Lindy made us take a nap. Did Patches win? How come you took so long? You said next time we came we could color. Dinner's ready, and you get to sit by both of us."

DJ felt like burying her head under her pillow. "Put a cork in it, guys." At the frown on her mother's face, DJ stopped trying to walk and peeled each twin off her leg and set them in front of her. "Now, give me a minute, okay?" At their nods, she continued, "No more questions."

They nodded again—in unison.

"Get to the table, boys. Joe, you and DJ want to wash up? Dinner is ready." Gran lifted a covered dish out of the oven. She set it on the counter and handed DJ a peanut-butter cookie. "That'll hold you till you get to the table."

At least it was quiet in the bathroom. DJ decided she'd never gripe about a quiet house again. She washed her hands and wiped a smudge off her cheek. Must have been a kiss from Major. Back down in the dining room, the boys patted the empty chair between them in case DJ didn't know where to sit.

Joe led the grace. "God is great, God is good, and we thank Him for our food." At the "Amen," one of the boys started to say something, but a look from Joe stopped it.

DJ promised herself she'd ask him how he did that.

Sunday after church, they all picked up Amy and went to the gallery where DJ's drawing hung on display.

"How come you didn't get the purple ribbon?"

"I like it better."

"So do I, guys, but an honorable mention isn't too bad." DJ studied the artwork around hers. She had to keep telling herself that.

"I like yours the best," Amy finally said after looking around. "All this other stuff is . . . is . . ." She turned to Gran. "What would you call it?"

"Modern art is as good a term as any. They were obviously looking for something unusual here." Gran stopped to study a sculpture.

"What do you think it is?" DJ whispered.

"It isn't what it is, but how it makes you feel." Gran turned to her with a smile.

"It makes *me* feel hungry."

"Oh, great—all my artist friend here can say is that it

makes her hungry." Amy danced away from DJ's threatening look.

"I think we'd better leave," Lindy said. "The boys are about to knock something over, and then where will we be?"

"Apologizing, most likely." Gran put two fingers in her mouth and whistled. Other visitors looked at her kind of strangely, but the boys came running back.

"You better teach me how to do that." Lindy curled a lock of hair behind her ear. "Or get me a leash."

"Well, I think you can be very proud, darlin'. Your drawing stands out among the rest of the works hanging here." Gran gave DJ a hug.

"She means yours is the only one that makes sense," Amy whispered with a giggle.

By Sunday night when Robert came for the twins, Lindy was the one who looked like she'd been caught under the six-horse hitch—and dragged.

10

"DID THE BOYS BEHAVE?"

"We was good, Daddy. Wasn't we?"

"Yes, of course." Lindy pushed back a strand of hair that had fallen across her forehead. She didn't even have any lipstick on, and she still wore the jeans she'd put on when they went to the park to play on the jungle gym. They'd stopped for hamburgers on their way home, and a smear of catsup decorated one pant leg.

DJ hung back and watched as Robert kissed Lindy, then bent down to hug and kiss the boys, who by now had glued themselves to his legs.

"Did you bring us a present, Daddy? Did you? Did you?"

"Shh, boys—in a minute." He looked at Lindy. "Sorry I'm late. We've been stacked up over northern California waiting for something to clear at the airport."

"Daddy!"

"No problem." Lindy swiped the hair back again.

DJ watched as the boys grew louder and her mother's lips tightened. Soon Robert took on the same harassed look Lindy wore.

"Well, see you guys. I got homework."

The twins threw themselves at her for hugs and kisses before returning to their father.

"What did you bring us? I want to go home. Will Nanny Jean be there?"

On one hand, DJ wanted to see the rest of the scene, and on the other, she had to leave before she burst out laughing. She didn't need a plan to prevent a wedding between her mother and Robert. All she had to do was let the twins loose. A short time later, she heard the front door close and Robert's car start and leave.

Her mother turned out the lights and made her way up the stairs and down the hall. She tapped on DJ's door. "Thanks for your help, dear. I never could have done it without you."

"Come on in." DJ lay flat on her bed, algebra book and notebook spread in front of her. *Dear.* Since when did her mother call her or anyone "dear"? *Things they are a'changing, that's for sure.*

"Are you behind on your homework?" Lindy leaned against the doorjamb.

"Not too bad. I worked ahead since I knew this weekend would be busy."

"Wish I could have done that."

"You decided on your thesis yet?" DJ found herself fishing for something to say. This was worse than being in a group of adults asking, "how's school?" or, "what do you want to do when you grow up?"

"I've narrowed it down to two projects. One might interest you."

DJ looked up from tracing the pattern in her bedspread.

"I'm thinking of focusing on teenage entrepreneurs, like you and Amy with the pony parties. I want to zero in on how kids start their own businesses and manage them. What do you think?"

"Your advisor would approve something like that?" DJ swung her feet to the floor.

Lindy nodded.

"Then I think it's cool."

"Do you know any other teens who've started their own businesses?"

DJ crossed one leg over her other knee and rested her elbows on her leg. "Not right off the bat, but I can ask at school. In fact, you could put an article or something in the school paper and let the kids contact you."

"If I did that at your school, maybe I could at others."

"I've seen articles in papers and magazines about kids and their businesses." DJ slid back on her bed and sat with her legs crossed. She patted the bed beside her. "You could check *Scholastic* or *Seventeen*. That would help you tap into kids from other areas."

"Do you read those magazines?"

"Sometimes."

"Hmm. And I thought you read only horse stuff." Lindy scraped at the catsup stain on her jeans. "You know, you're really good with the twins."

"Thanks."

"They like you."

"They like anyone who answers their questions." *Where is this conversation going? What am I supposed to say now? They like you, too?*

"Well, I better get to bed. I'll set up a search on the Internet tomorrow and see if I can find more kids who have businesses of their own. I can use you and Amy for a case study, can't I?"

DJ nodded. "Sure."

"And some of your other attempts, too?"

"M-o-m, get real."

"No, I'm serious. I need failed attempts, too, and yours are good examples of learning by trial and error."

"Yeah, mostly error." DJ looked up at her mother, one eyebrow raised. "You're kidding, right?"

Lindy shook her head. "And if the thesis works out well,

I'm thinking of using the research to write a book. What do you think of that?"

"Wow. That's really cool."

"That's also just a dream. Thanks for all the help." Lindy started to walk out. "Oh, DJ? I'm sorry you didn't do better in the show. I hope having the twins there didn't affect your performance."

"Yeah, well, I have to learn to deal with distractions and the unexpected. At least that's what Bridget keeps drilling into me. I'm glad you came."

"Me too." As Lindy left the room, a breath of her perfume lingered on the air.

DJ sniffed. How come Gran's roses still smelled so much better? "Night, Mom."

Later, as she lay trying to go to sleep, DJ thought back over the conversation with her mother. DJ and Amy in a thesis? What would Amy say?

When DJ got home from school on Monday, the house was still a shambles from the weekend. She wandered out to the backyard that used to be such a showplace. Now, dead flowers and seed pods covered more of the plants than blossoms. The roses needed pruning. She tried to pull a carrot to munch, but the ground was so dry the top broke off.

"Fiddle." She dug down into the dirt and yanked out the carrot. She washed it under the faucet and turned on the sprinklers. They needed to get automatic ones at this rate. Now DJ couldn't leave till the yard was soaked. She shook her head. She'd have to remember to turn them on when she got home and off again.

"Even the hummingbird feeders are empty. Just like me." She shook her head. Here she was talking to herself.

And yesterday she'd been praying for quiet.

Joe and Ranger were in the ring when she and Amy arrived at the Academy. Tony had the jumping arena. His horse wore the dark sheen of hard work, and Tony's face wore a frown.

"Did you hear what his father said to him yesterday?" Amy asked as they ambled toward the tack room.

"Nope." DJ picked Patches' bridle off the peg.

"Well, let's just say I know where the kid gets it."

DJ stopped before picking up a grooming bucket. "Gets what?"

"The way he talks to Hilary." Amy dropped her voice. "If my father talked to me that way, I'd . . . I'd . . . I don't know what I'd do, but it would be bad."

"Ames, quit yakking in circles and tell me. What did the man say?"

"He yelled at Tony for letting a—you know, the *n* word—beat him. He said if Tony couldn't do better than that, they'd sell his horse and he could go play Pogs with the little kids."

DJ sank down on the bench. "How come you didn't tell me sooner?"

Amy shrugged. "No time. And you weren't in a very good mood, if you remember. That man used more four-letter words than the creeps do at school. If I talked like that, I'd be grounded for life."

"Me too." DJ gnawed on her lower lip. "All I know is that if things don't change soon, Hilary will leave. If anyone's gonna leave, it ought to be Tony."

They both picked up their buckets and started down the aisle.

"DJ."

She turned to see Bridget coming toward them. "What's up?"

"I need to know if you are going to the jumping clinic at Wild Horse Ranch. The registrations need to be in the mail today."

DJ rubbed her bottom lip with her tongue. "I guess not. I really need a saddle, so I'm saving all my money for that."

"Sorry to hear that. It is not often one is given the opportunity to work with someone of this instructor's caliber."

"I'd just like to meet the man. Seeing a former Olympic rider in person—that's better than meeting any movie star."

"Well, maybe next time."

"Maybe next time what?" Joe, leading Ranger, walked up to the trio.

After DJ explained the situation, Joe just shook his head. "I'll pay the fee. Why didn't you tell me? You know Gran says all you have to do is ask."

"I know, but Robert volunteered and Mom wouldn't let him. I figured I better leave well enough alone."

To go or not to go. The choices warred in DJ's head. So what if her mother got mad at her—it wouldn't be anything new. Was the jumping clinic worth a fight? Lindy hadn't exactly said DJ couldn't go—she'd just said Robert couldn't pay and that DJ needed to earn the money. This wasn't exactly earning the money, but she had found it another way. And Joe was right, Gran *had* said she'd pay for DJ's showing fees, but that was when she lived in the same house. Did the offer still stand?

"DJ, let me worry about Lindy, okay?" Joe dug his wallet out of his pocket. "How much is it?"

"Thanks, GJ. I'll pay you back somehow."

He pulled out several more bills. "How about if I go, too? I'm sure I could learn plenty since I'm such a novice. This way, I'll know what you are talking about."

"Good idea." Bridget nodded. "You will find there are clinics for cutting horses, too, in case you decide to train Ranger yourself."

"I better get going. Thanks again, GJ, and you, too, Bridget." DJ picked up her gear and danced down the row until she came to Patches' stall. The gelding nickered when he saw her. "Hey, that's a first." She dug in her bucket for a couple of horse cookies. "Here's your treat. I better remind your mother to bring them to you since you're such a sweetie today." The horse tossed his head, spraying her with slobber and bits of grain. "And then again, maybe not." She wiped her face and set to work with the brushes.

By the time she'd worked Patches' energy off so he could get down to business, she'd used up half of her time with him. Obviously his owner hadn't been out to ride him today. DJ couldn't get used to the idea that people who owned horses didn't ride them every day. In fact, some of the stabled horses were never ridden except by academy employees.

"Why have a horse if you don't ride him?" Patches shook his head. He pulled at the bit as if hoping DJ had forgotten to let him run.

"No, you have to mind. Then we can play." She kept her aids firm, insisting that he move away from the pressure of a leg. Every time he obeyed, she rewarded him with pats and praise. "Remind me to tell Mrs. Johnson to lunge you or let you at it on the hot walker before she gets on. No wonder you can buffalo her—you just have too much energy."

By the time she'd put him away and taken Major out, she felt like she'd been sitting on a jackhammer. When she put Major into an easy trot, it felt as though she were sitting on a pillow. What a difference a well-behaved horse could make!

"He learned to conserve his energy when he was on the

force," Joe said from the sidelines. "He knew there was a long day ahead."

"He's smart all right. That's why he's learning so fast." DJ rode over to the side and stopped. "You on your way home now?"

He nodded.

"Give Gran a hug for me. Tell her the cookie jar is empty."

"Yeah, sure. The one at my house comes first, kid."

DJ watched for a moment as he strode across the lot to his Explorer. While she was glad Joe and Gran were so happy, she sure wished Gran would be at home for her like she used to, with dinner waiting and a clean house. The comforting smell of turpentine and oil paints was almost gone, and it had been far too long for the delicious smell of cookies to linger.

"Back to work, big fella." She spoke to cover the lump that blossomed in her throat.

Lights on meant Lindy was home. DJ pedaled faster and parked her bike in the garage, then closed the automatic door. "Hey, Mom?"

No answer. The kitchen wore a half-clean look, and the family room could stand a clutter check. DJ reminded herself to turn on the sprinklers. Then she ambled up the stairs. A glance in her mother's bedroom told the story. Lindy lay with a cloth over her eyes—a sure sign of a migraine headache.

DJ tiptoed to the edge of the bed. "Can I get you anything?"

"No, thanks." Lindy spoke without moving her lips.

DJ knew then that it was a bad one. She sighed and reached over to unplug the phone.

"Robert has something to show us. He'll be here Saturday morning about ten."

"I won't be here. I've got that jumping clinic up in Napa. I told you about it."

"Oh."

DJ hoped her mother would let it go at that.

"Call him, then, so we can make other arrangements."

"Sure." DJ took a deep breath of relief. "I'll check on you later in case you want some soup or something."

"Thank you."

DJ closed the door gently and made her way downstairs. After slicing a piece of cheese, she dialed Robert's number. "Hi, Mom said to call you. I'm going to that jumping clinic in Napa on Saturday, so we—or at least, I—won't be here."

"Good, I'm glad you're going. Decided to take money out for it, huh?"

"Well, no. Joe paid for both me and him." *And please don't tell my mother,* she wanted to say, but then . . . things were becoming a tangled mess.

"Oh, okay. How about Sunday after church? The boys and I could go to your church, and then we'll have brunch out before I show you the surprise."

"Ah . . . well . . . you know my mom doesn't like surprises. I think I take after her."

"Well, I think she'll like this one—at least I hope so. Tell her I'll call her tomorrow. Oh, DJ, does she get headaches like this very often?"

DJ thought a moment. "Maybe once a month or so. I guess I never paid much attention to how often." After hanging up the phone, she thought about the surprise Robert had in store. He sure sounded excited. She hoped her mother would like it.

She'd just finished making tomato soup and a grilled-cheese sandwich when the phone rang.

It was Gran. "DJ, I have a problem," she began. "I need some horses for a new book I'm working on, and your horses are usually better than mine. How about drawing some for me, then I'll paint them in?"

"Sure, but when do you need them?"

"Yesterday. I took this project knowing it would be a tight deadline. The artist they originally hired took sick, and they need it as soon as I can get it to them."

"I could come over each night after I work at the Academy." Without touching the floor, or at least it seemed that way, DJ danced across the room after hanging up the phone. She was going to help Gran out. Her horses would be in a children's book! If only she could call Amy, but it was too late.

She took her tomato soup and grilled-cheese sandwich up to her room so she could look through her sketches. Maybe one or some of them might work. Or maybe she could make them work.

The house was still a mess when she came down in the morning. She'd planned to straighten up, but she'd gotten so involved in the drawings, she'd gone to bed late. A horn honked from the drive. Amy was already here. She'd have to take time to do it before she headed for the Academy.

The light was blinking on the machine. That would wait, too. Out the door she flew.

DJ's art teacher stopped her before she left class.

"I was really pleased to see you got that honorable mention at the art show. Have you thought of taking some extra art classes after school or on the weekends? You have real talent."

"Thank you, but all my time is taken up at the Academy where I work and stable my horse. I really don't have any spare time right now." DJ fidgeted from one foot to another. Mrs. Yamamoto was waiting for her.

"I think horses are great, but art classes could make a difference in what you choose to do with the rest of your life. Why don't you have your mother give me a call?"

"Sure, thanks. I'm late for my ride." DJ took the slip of paper and dashed off to her locker. She had so much to do, and now she was already late.

She listened to the waiting message while she got out peanut butter and jelly for a sandwich.

"DJ, you left the sprinklers on all night. You know what that will do to our water bill?"

DJ groaned. And she didn't have time to do her chores, either. She threw the dishes into the dishwasher, then grabbed the books, crayons, and paper in the family room and stuffed them under a cushion—the rest would have to wait. Out the door. Back inside. Upstairs to get her drawings for Gran. Out the door. Back inside. She needed a sweat shirt. The clouds were already edging the tops of the Briones hills.

"You're late," Amy scolded.

"Don't I know it." The girls pedaled as though they were in a race.

Joe met her at the tack room. "DJ, was Major limping last night?"

"No, why?"

"There's some swelling in his right front leg. I've been icing it, but you better not ride him for a few days. He must have pulled a muscle."

DJ felt her stomach thud down to her ankles. What had she done now?

DJ CHARGED OUT TO MAJOR'S STALL. "Hey, fella, what's happening with you?" She ran her hand down his leg. Sure enough—hot to the touch and puffy. "Do you think we need to call the vet?"

"No. I have some liniment, and with that and the ice, he'll be fine," Joe said.

"You're sure? Did Bridget see him yet? Oh, Major, I'm so sorry." The horse snuffled DJ's hair and searched her pockets for treats. He blew in her face when he found nothing. "Sorry, no time to stop for cookies. Joe here scared the thought right out of me."

"I'm afraid it means no jumping clinic on Saturday."

"But what could have caused it? He didn't hit a pole or anything."

"Did he stumble?"

"Not that I can think of." DJ squatted down to inspect the swelling again. She ran gentle hands over the area. "Joe, I wouldn't hurt him for anything."

"I know. These things happen. Maybe he just figures he needs a rest. It's not your fault."

"I should have checked him more carefully when I put him away. Didn't I cool him down enough? Is that it?"

Joe lifted her up and set her on her feet. "DJ, look at me.

Watch my mouth move. It is not, I repeat—*not*—your fault. No matter how hard you try, you can't take care of the entire world. Or take responsibility for it, for that matter. Now, go about your chores and we'll leave early for a scrumptious dinner. You earned a break as much as Major did."

"A break? Could it be a stress fracture?"

"Help!" Joe shook his head. "I won't even dignify that with an answer. I'll see you in a while. You go practice concentration with your students and Patches."

"But I . . ."

"Go."

"Maybe I should spend the night here so I can ice him again."

"Go."

DJ started to follow his instructions and stopped. "If you talk to Bridget right away, maybe you can get your money back for the clinic on Saturday. Or you *could* go without me."

"No chance. I'll talk to her—now get."

DJ managed to check on Major three times over the afternoon, and each time the leg looked the same. She wrinkled her nose at the smell of the liniment. The last time, Joe had applied the ice boot again, and Major looked as though he wore a padded sleeve over his leg.

The big horse stood contentedly munching his evening ration of grain and hay. She gave him another hug and a kiss on the soft skin of his nose.

"See you tomorrow. You be good now." She turned to Joe. "Maybe I should—"

"Get in the truck. Gran is waiting dinner on us."

DJ and Gran lost themselves in planning the horse drawings for the book. They didn't even look up when the phone rang.

"DJ, it's for you." Joe held out the receiver.

"Oh no." DJ knew she was in trouble. "I forgot to leave a message for Mom about where I'd be." She held the phone away from her ear to soften the cutting tones of her mother's voice. "But, Mom—" She couldn't get a word in edgewise as she was reminded again about how irresponsible it was to leave the water running all night.

Joe stood when she hung up. "I'll take you home."

"I'd rather stay here." DJ could feel her anger burning as fast as a fire built with dry kindling. "It's just not fair. No matter how hard I try, it's never good enough. Gran, I miss you so much." She dropped to her knees by her grandmother's chair and laid her head in the soft lap.

"I know, darlin'. But you and your mom have been doing pretty well lately." Gran stroked the wisps of hair back from DJ's forehead.

"Yeah, we get along really well when we never see each other." DJ could feel the anger dwindling with each stroke of her grandmother's hand.

"Lindy will do better once her thesis subject is approved. She's worked long and hard for this degree. It means a lot to her."

"More than I do."

"No, that's not true. I know you feel that way sometimes, and I understand. But your mother loves you—she just doesn't know how to show it."

"Yeah, well, yelling at me sure doesn't cut it." DJ looked at the folder of drawings resting on the table. "I better get home. I didn't get my homework done, either, so I hope she doesn't ask."

"That's my fault. We were having too good a time." Gran dropped a kiss on DJ's hair. "I'll tell her we need to do this all week. She'll understand—she was just worried about you."

"Where else would I be?" DJ got to her feet. "Thanks for dinner. Sorry I didn't help with the dishes."

"Oh, that's nothing. Our art was far more important." Gran walked DJ and Joe to the door. "I can always do the dishes."

"Or I can." Joe winked at DJ. "I *do* do dishes, you know."

Lindy was on the phone by the time DJ walked in. She could tell Robert was on the other end by the soft sound of Lindy's voice, not at all like the one she'd used to call DJ.

"Night, Mom." DJ waved and got a nod back. Too tired to do any homework, she crawled into bed and fell asleep on the *a* of amen.

Because she couldn't train Major, DJ had extra time that week to work on the drawings Gran needed. Each night they sketched, erased, and finally transferred the illustrations to stretched canvas so Gran could paint them. DJ particularly loved one they'd done of a young foal with furry ears and a brush of a mane.

Lindy left a message that they'd be going with Robert to see the surprise on Saturday since DJ didn't have the clinic.

DJ was spending Friday night at Gran's, and the two of them were working in the studio. "Why can't Mom ask me about *my* schedule before she plans things for *us* to do? Joe said I can ride Major again tomorrow, but only at a walk. He did fine on the lunge line tonight."

DJ studied the horse's head they were pairing with that of the little girl who was the heroine in the story. It made an attractive logo. If this book did well, the publisher was considering turning it into a series. "I really like this. I wish I could draw people as good as you do."

"And I wish my horses had as much life as yours." Gran held up the last drawing. "You have a real gift, darlin'."

"Well, I got it from you. Did I tell you my teacher said I should take art lessons?"

"No. That's exciting news."

"I said no. I don't have time right now." At the sad look on Gran's face, DJ added, "You know riding is more important to me than anything. I just can't do one more thing. If I mess up again, Mom will ground me forever."

"Just remember, if you decide you might like to take art classes, the money will be there."

Joe looked up from the book he was reading. "The same goes for riding clinics, shows, and riding lessons should you need training beyond what Bridget can offer you."

DJ blinked a couple of times to dry her eyes. "Thanks. You two are the best."

Gran turned back to the drawings spread across the table. She lifted one of a month-old colt. "I think this one needs some work on that off hind leg, then we can use him for page eight. What do you think?"

DJ picked up her art-gum eraser. "You're right. The ears need some work, too." The quiet of concentration came to rest on the room.

Some time later, the phone rang.

"It's for you, DJ." Joe held out the receiver. "Your mother," he mouthed.

"I just wanted to remind you to be back home and cleaned up by eleven tomorrow."

"I know." DJ held the phone away from her face and stared at the receiver, shaking her head. "She hung up. She must still be upset." DJ returned to the table. *That I can do without*. She could feel the resentment bubble. *Who needs her?*

She caught the look that passed between Joe and Gran.

"Do you know what's going on?"

"Robert wants it to be a surprise. We won't spoil it for him." Gran shook her head when DJ started to interrupt.

"Nope, I won't even give you a hint."

"Ah, come on, Gran." DJ put her best wheedle into her voice.

"No way."

DJ hurried through Saturday morning chores so she had plenty of time to walk Major around the soft sand of the arena.

"You act as if you never had a problem at all," she said, leaning forward to stroke his neck. Major moved smoothly beneath her, not favoring the injured leg in the least. DJ thought about the clinic going on up in Napa. Both Tony and Hilary had gone up for it, along with a couple of the adults who stabled their horses and rode at the Academy.

The sun was breaking out of the early morning fog, and DJ lifted her face to its warmth. "I'd rather be riding up in the hills, wouldn't you?" Major snorted and lifted his feet a bit higher, as if hoping she would relent and let him trot.

"Sure would." Joe rode up beside her. Ranger didn't appreciate walking any more than Major.

"Then let's. The trail wouldn't be too hard and . . ."

"And you have to be ready at eleven. You know that if we got started, we wouldn't want to turn back."

"I know. Am I gonna like the surprise?" DJ clutched her reins, willing herself to remain calm. She deliberately loosened her fingers and relaxed her wrists. With the release of a deep breath, she turned her head to look at her grandfather.

"I hope so, DJ, I surely hope so."

DJ kept his words in mind as she put Major away and climbed onto her bike to ride home.

Robert and the boys were already there. "No, you're not

late," he reassured her when she glanced at her watch. "We're early."

"DJ, we's gonna see—" Robert clapped his hands over both twins' mouths.

"Remember, this is a secret. A surprise." Robert squatted down so he was on eye level with the bouncing Bs. "You promised not to tell."

They both nodded, blue eyes bright above his fingers. When he removed his hands, they flung themselves at DJ's legs.

She bent down to hug them. How could anyone resist the adoration shining in their faces? "I'll be ready in a few minutes." She headed for the stairs. When they started to follow her, she sent a pleading look at Robert.

"Come on, guys, we'll wait here while DJ dresses. She's not used to an audience."

"We can help."

"I'm sure you can, but we'll read a story instead while we wait." Robert took them by the hands and over to the sofa.

DJ fled up the stairs as they clamored for their favorite story. Strange, her mother wasn't downstairs pacing the floor, making noises like DJ should hurry. Did Lindy know what the surprise was? Was she unhappy about it? Questions, questions.

Robert herded the boys to the car as soon as DJ leaped down the stairs. She looked at her mother but saw nothing other than a gracious smile on her face. The headache lines were gone. With the boys buckled into their seat belts, DJ sat back and tried to unwind. She knew she could get the twins to tell her about the surprise, but that wouldn't be fair. Robert wanted to surprise them.

He stopped at the stop sign and turned right, the same way DJ rode every day to the Academy. They drove past the Academy, then passed Gran and Joe's. DJ looked down to see the Double Bs with their hands clapped over their mouths. What was going on?

A quarter of a mile beyond Gran's house, Robert turned into a tree-shaded driveway. They stopped beside a white house with brick halfway up the front and friendly windows.

"What do you think of it?" Robert shut off the ignition and turned to Lindy.

"It's a nice house, I guess." Lindy looked up at him. "Pretty yard."

"Let's go see the inside."

The boys threw off their seat belts and exploded out the door. At a shake of their father's head, they ran in place until they could grab DJ's hands and pull her toward the front door. A fan-shaped window over the door caught her eye.

Instead of knocking, Robert unlocked the door. Strange. One didn't go unlocking someone else's house. They obviously weren't coming here to visit someone.

They entered an empty living room with vaulted ceilings—a fireplace ran clear to the ceiling on one wall, and an abundance of windows let in the outdoors.

"What do you think?" Robert had his arm around Lindy's shoulders.

"It's beautiful." Lindy stood very still, her eyes trained on the wide stair that curved up to the second floor.

"I thought so, too—that's why I bought it. The place has five acres and a barn with horse stalls. Though the house isn't large enough now, it will be by the time my men get finished with it. I figure we could move in by March . . . that is, if you think a February wedding would be about right?"

"Robert, I . . ."

"Let me show you the rest of the place." He took Lindy's arm and led her through an arch to another room.

DJ felt as though she'd been kicked in the head by a one-ton draft horse. Robert had bought them a house! *He* certainly was convinced they could become a family. But her mother hadn't said yes yet—had she?

DJ could ignore the dynamos tugging at her arms no longer. She let them pull her up the stairs, down the stairs, out to the kitchen, and to the backyard, but she needed no encouragement to visit the barn. Four stalls, a board-fenced paddock, and a field for grazing. She turned and looked at the house. Robert wanted to make it *bigger*?

"Daddy said we could have two ponies, and Major can live here, too." The boys ran from stall to stall, opening each half door and chasing each other inside and out again.

DJ tried to tune them out so she could think clearly. Had her mother agreed to this? She shook her head. No, Lindy had been as surprised as her daughter, DJ realized, remembering the shocked look on her mother's face.

"Come on, guys, let's go see what's happening at the house." She turned and headed out of the barn, sure they would follow.

"Daddy said we could have a dog here, too. Two dogs, even. You want one? I want a pony now." The two overlapped comments as usual. "When we gonna move, DJ? You're the best sister in the whole world!"

DJ sensed the icy chill the moment she stepped through the sliding-glass door into the breakfast area. Uh-oh, her mother was not happy. DJ put a finger to her lips to shush the boys before they charged into the house.

"But, Robert, I didn't say I'd marry you."

"But you've said that you love me. This just doesn't make sense."

"I know, but marriage is a big step. It's a lot to think about, and it's not fair to pressure me by buying this house."

"Lindy, honey, this isn't pressure. I'd have bought this house even if it were just for the boys and me. It's near Dad and Gran, the boys can have a dog and ponies, and I'm building more houses out in this area now. I can move my office out of the city and not have to commute."

DJ put her hands over the twin mouths about to erupt beside her. She shook her head and whispered, "Be quiet, okay?" The boys nodded, so she removed her hands and took theirs. Together, they tiptoed back outside and sat down on the redwood steps.

So many things to think about. She stared out at the barn. She could have Major right at home with her. She wouldn't have to work at the Academy all the time to pay for his board and keep. She'd ride over there for lessons. There was room in the field for jumps. The boys could ride in the paddock until they got good enough to ride up in the hills.

And DJ would have a father—and two brothers. She watched the boys kneeling on the ground, studying something in the grass.

"DJ, come here." One of them waved to her.

"DJ, boys, come on. Let's go eat." Robert stopped in the doorway.

DJ got to her feet. Robert sure did have a knack for surprises. When DJ found her mother in the living room, traces of tears still glistened in her mother's slightly red eyes.

What had her answer been?

12

"WHAT DO YOU THINK, DJ?"

"What do you mean, what do I think? About what?" DJ stalled for time. She knew her mother was talking about Robert. *It's not fair. Don't ask me. I'm just a kid, remember—that's what you're always telling me.*

Lindy sat curled up in Gran's wing chair, one hand propping up her head. The lamplight glinted on the auburn tints in her hair and made it shine blood bay.

The phone rang, and DJ leaped to her feet. "I'll get it."

"If it's Robert, tell him I'm not home."

"Sure, she's right here." DJ leaned around the corner. "It's for you."

"Who is it?" Lindy mouthed. DJ shook her head and shrugged.

DJ left her mother talking and headed for her room. How could she give her mother an answer when she had no idea what she thought? And asking her daughter to lie for her? Of course, it had been Gran who had always insisted on telling the truth. Lindy had never been home.

DJ got out her sketch book and pencil box, taking time to sharpen each tip to perfection. After building her nest on the bed, she soon lost herself in a world of lines and shading. The foal she and Gran had been working with slowly appeared on the paper. Trying to get the ears just right, she erased one and started again.

A loud knock at the door finally got her attention. "Yeah?"

"May I come in?"

"Sure." DJ heaved a sigh. Why couldn't she be left alone to draw? Life was so much easier when all she had to think about was sketching and shading. Draw and approve or erase. No major decisions.

"That was my boss. I'll be leaving tomorrow morning for a three-day trip to Los Angeles. Mom said it was okay for you to stay there."

"Great."

Lindy paused, as if waiting for DJ to say something else. "Fine, then. I better get packed. Good night."

"Night, Mom. Have a good trip." When the door closed again, DJ thumped her fist on the pillow. "Yes!" Three days with Gran and Joe—and without her mother.

Tuesday morning Robert called before DJ left for school. She answered the phone with a questioning look at Gran, who shrugged in return. What could Robert be calling *her* for?

"You want to take *me* out to dinner? Why?"

"I'd like to get to know you better. We never get time to talk when all the others are around."

DJ tipped her head to the side. "Well, I guess."

"Good, I'll pick you up at seven, if that's all right."

DJ hung up the phone and turned to Joe and Gran, who were sitting at the breakfast table. "What'll we talk about?"

Joe laughed. "I think you'll find Robert is an entertaining companion, if you give him a chance."

"There's a message there, darlin'." Gran took another sip of her coffee.

DJ picked up her backpack and slung it over one shoulder. "We gotta go, GJ, or I'll be late."

Monday was the day she got to spend the most time with Major, but since his leg prevented them from jumping yet, they worked on the flat instead. DJ posted till she felt her legs turn to cooked spaghetti. She concentrated on each of her aids—hands, legs, and feet—but especially on how she held her head. She'd never realized how often she looked down or off to the side. Keeping Major going straight was one problem, but the more crucial one was her concentration.

They crossed the cavalletti so many times she felt pole happy. Major seemed to enjoy every minute of it, striding with ears forward, neck arched, and snorting every once in a while.

After walking him out, DJ checked the leg to make sure there was no swelling. "You're a trooper, you are." She stroked the horse's neck and rubbed his ears. "We'll probably be able to jump on Wednesday. What do you think?"

Major snorted and bobbed his head. She checked his hay net and the water bucket, then got his grain. "I'd much rather stay here with you than go to dinner with Robert. Why doesn't he just come to Gran's for dinner?"

Joe appeared at the stall opening. "Because he wants time with you, not us. You ready to go?"

"Where would you like to eat?" Robert asked once they were in his car heading for the road. "What kind of food do you like?"

"Chinese, Italian, Mexican—pretty much anything but Thai, it's too spicy." DJ looked over at the man driving. "I'm not particular. What do you like?"

"All of the above. How about we go somewhere you don't go often?"

That won't be hard, DJ thought. *We never go out except for hamburgers or pizza*. "Italian then?"

"Fine. How about Giannini's?"

When they were seated in a booth with a white tablecloth and their hostess had lighted the low candle, DJ looked around. Robert had good taste in restaurants—now if only the food lived up to the decor.

"I know the ravioli is delicious, and the pastas are superb. They make their own." Robert smiled at the waiter, who wore a black tie and spoke with a heavy Italian accent. "What do you want to drink, DJ? I'm having iced tea."

"That'll be fine." DJ looked up when the waiter lifted the crown-shaped napkin from her plate, shook it, and laid it across her lap. "Ah, thank you." She glanced over to catch a smile on Robert's face. She raised her eyebrows and smiled back.

By the time they'd ordered, she couldn't begin to explain why she'd been uptight about dinner with Robert. He made her laugh and got her to tell him all about her early days at the Academy—and the disastrous times she and Amy had tried to earn money.

"And the hamsters got loose in the garage?"

"Actually, some of them were in my bedroom. One even got into Mom's." DJ rolled her tongue in the side of her cheek. "She can yell pretty loudly when a creepy critter gets too close."

Robert went from a chuckle to an outright laugh, a deep sound that made other people turn to see who was having such a good time.

"Did you catch them all?"

"Finally. I sold them to a friend whose brother had a six-foot boa constrictor. He was always looking for snake food."

Their dinner was everything Robert had promised. DJ knew that from then on, she'd be partial to ravioli. The dessert tray looked like an artist had been painting dreams. She chose something called chocolate decadence and wished she could eat such creamy chocolate every night.

When Robert ordered coffee, she leaned back into her chair and gave serious thought to unbuttoning the waistband of her twill dress pants.

"Tell me about your dream of being on the Olympic team."

"That's what I'm trying for." DJ leaned her elbows on the table.

"No, I mean, what will it take? I have no idea how a person ends up on the U.S. equestrian team."

"Well, you need to qualify, just like for all the other sports. I'd have to be known for winning shows—the big shows where you earn points. Olympic riders have really top-notch horses—hot bloods like Thoroughbreds—and both the horse and rider undergo tremendous training."

"Sounds expensive."

"It is. It's also one of the few events where age doesn't count. In fact, rarely is someone under twenty-five admitted to the team." DJ moved her spoon around. "I know I can do it, though. Gran says that if you want something bad enough and pray hard and work hard for it, you can do it. I've been working and praying as hard as I can, so I figure God will help me. At least, that's what Gran says. She teaches me Bible verses so I know where to turn for encouragement."

"Well, I'd like to be one of those who helps you, too. You have a big dream, DJ, and I admire people who are willing to work hard for their dreams."

"Thank you."

Once back in the car, Robert asked, "What did you think of my new house?"

"It's nice."

"Did Lindy tell you what I plan to do with it?"

DJ shook her head. "Mom and I haven't talked a lot since then."

"She's upset, isn't she?"

DJ shrugged. How was she supposed to answer that?

"Look, DJ, I know you weren't exactly pleased at first with the idea of me marrying your mother. I'm hoping that's changed, because I really want us all to be together. I love your mother, and I know she loves me. If we all work at it, we'll make a wonderful family. And after I finish the remodeling, that house will be a great place for all of us. You can have what is now the master bedroom and bath for your own, and the boys will share the other. The new wing will have a master-bedroom suite, an office for me, and probably a playroom. I'm not sure yet."

He looked over at DJ. "I'm trying to give you a sales job, aren't I?"

"You didn't mention the horse barn yet." DJ grinned at him. "The boys already told me they were going to take riding lessons."

"Yeah, ponies and dogs are all they think about." He turned into Gran's driveway. "Sometime I'd like to hear what you think about this wedding. Thanks for the date. I really enjoyed myself."

"So did I." DJ climbed out of the car. "Tell the boys hi for me. And thank you for the yummy dinner."

"Did you have a good time?" Gran asked as DJ stepped in the door.

"Yeah, I did. He's a really nice person." DJ yawned. "I better get to bed. Gran, I been thinking—if I could work Major mornings before school, I'd have more time in the afternoon and evening for all the other stuff I have to do. What do you think?"

Gran shook her head. "I think that's asking too much of yourself."

"Other Olympic contenders do it—why not me?"

"But why not?" DJ carefully kept any trace of a whine out of her voice. She had asked her mother to discuss the idea of early morning workouts again, and acting like a little kid wouldn't help her cause. While her mother had said no several months before, maybe now would be different. DJ certainly hoped so.

"DJ, you have too much to do already." Lindy paced the family room. "You'd have to ride up to the Academy in the dark, and I won't permit that."

"You could give me a ride on your way to work."

"But you'd go to school smelling like a horse. No, that just won't work."

"Please, Mom. Just think about it, okay?"

"DJ, no. I haven't changed my mind. I cannot give you permission to ride in the morning, and that's that. You are only fourteen, and you need your rest. You'd have to be in bed by eight to keep going, and you know how you like to stay up late."

"I can change." DJ bit her lip to keep angry words from spilling out.

"We won't discuss this anymore. Just keep up your chores and your grades—that's all I ask. Your life at the Academy is your choice. You have your horse now, can't you be satisfied?"

"No, I can't. You always have money for the things you want, like school and another degree. Just because I don't want the same things you do, you won't help me. You don't care."

"Darla Jean Randall—"

"Don't bother to say it. I'm going." She spun away and dashed up the stairs to her room. Just in time, she kept from slamming the door. She flung herself across the bed and pounded her fists on the mattress. Her eyes burned and her throat closed. She *would not* cry. She would not! Only babies cried.

How come her mother could be so selfish? She didn't care about anything but herself. DJ thumped her fist again in rhythm with her thoughts. *Why? I know she hates me. She isn't like a mother—Gran is more my mother. It isn't fair!*

After a time of thumping and muttering her angry thoughts, DJ rolled over onto her back and stared at the ceiling. Why couldn't she stay cool and calm like she'd planned? Fighting never did any good.

She could hear the water running in her mother's bathroom. Lindy was brushing her teeth. What would happen if DJ went in there and demanded she be allowed to ride in the morning?

Dumb idea.

What if she went in and said she was sorry? But sorry for what? For asking for what she wanted? That's what Gran had said to do—ask. Of course, Gran had meant she should ask God and Gran; she never mentioned asking Lindy.

DJ chewed on the cuticle of her thumb. What if her mother came in here and kissed her good-night and said I love you, like Gran used to do? She brushed the sides of her eyes and swallowed—hard.

The next afternoon at the Academy, she was back to

square one with Andrew. Suddenly, he didn't want to brush Bandit, he didn't want to feed Bandit, he didn't even want to be in the stall with the pony.

"What's happened, Andrew? I thought you were beginning to like Bandit."

"No. I want to go home."

Short of dragging him into the stall, DJ didn't know what to do. "You want to come see Major?" A head shake. "How about saying hello to Patches? We could stand back a ways." Another shake. The boy's lower lip stuck out, and his chin wobbled. DJ sank down against the wall and patted the shavings next to her. "Come sit here with me. We have to talk."

Keeping one eye on the pony who stood in front of the hay net pulling out wisps of hay and munching, the little boy joined DJ, copying her cross-legged pose.

"Now, the way I see it, your job is to groom Bandit here. He's never hurt you."

"But, he scared me."

"I know, but it wasn't on purpose. He was swatting flies. I need to put fly spray on him so the flies don't bother him. How would you like flies crawling on your legs and in your eyes?"

The boy shuddered. "Yuk."

"So let's get with the program and get this pony groomed. Then we can put fly spray on him." She got to her feet and extended a hand. Andrew let her pull him up.

With a look that said he thought she was killing him, he took the brush and started brushing.

Please, God, don't let Bandit frighten him again. Help this kid get over his fear and please show me how to help, too. DJ kept brushing, praying, and teasing Andrew until he finally laughed at one of her jokes.

By the end of their session, they had one clean pony and one boy who'd overcome enough fear to keep going.

"You know, Andrew, you are one brave guy." DJ held the bucket while he filled it with grooming gear.

"Why?"

"'Cause even though you're afraid, you keep on trying. That's pretty neat, don't you think?"

"I guess."

His mother met them with her arm in a sling.

"What happened to you?" DJ asked.

"Andrew, why don't you go get in the car. I'll be right there." Mrs. Johnson sent her son on the way with a pat on the shoulder. She turned to DJ. "I fell off Patches and wrenched my shoulder. Andrew was scared again today, wasn't he?"

DJ nodded. "But we got through it. Tough about getting hurt. Falls happen a lot with horses. Did Patches act up?"

"He spooked at something, and I just wasn't ready. I probably wasn't paying close enough attention."

"Too bad. Well, take care of your arm, and I'll make sure Patches gets the steam worked off. You're putting him on the hot walker or lunging him first, aren't you?"

"Usually, but that time I didn't. I was in a hurry." Mrs. Johnson shook her head. "I had to learn a lesson, I guess. See you."

DJ wandered back into the barn. She could hear raised voices coming from the south aisle of the barn. She stopped to listen. The drawl and the words being used indicated one voice could only be Tony Andrada's. DJ felt like a rampaging mother bear whose cub had been attacked. What right had he to talk to Hilary like that—Hilary, who wouldn't hurt an ant?

DJ stormed down the aisle, but by the time she reached the stall, Tony had made it out the door and Hilary had disappeared.

DJ checked all the stalls. No Hilary. She looked in the tack room and trotted across to the office, but it was locked. Even Bridget was gone. Back in the barn, she thought for a moment. The haystack!

Hilary was wiping away her tears when DJ approached.

"I swear, I could hit him over the head with a shovel." DJ sank down on a bale of hay.

"It wouldn't do any good. He's as hardheaded as they come. It isn't just that I'm black, either—he thinks all women should do his work for him. I bet his mother still butters his toast."

"And picks up his dirty socks."

"Makes his bed. She'd probably breathe for him if she could." The two girls shared a bit of a smile at their jokes.

"Have you said anything to Bridget?" DJ rested her arms on her knees.

Hilary shook her head. "But I don't think I can put up with this much longer. I've found another stable that will take my horse, and their trainer is okay." She straightened her back and took a deep breath. "If I could only keep him from getting to me. My father says to ignore him, and, DJ, I try. I really try. But he just won't quit. And to make matters worse, he doesn't finish his chores and tries to get by without doing a good job. You know Bridget trains us all to do everything correctly. We don't allow slipshod work here."

"Until Tony." DJ swung her clasped hands. "James wasn't always the greatest worker, either, but he was younger and he came around. And he didn't have a father who hammered racist garbage into his head."

"You heard Tony?"

DJ nodded. "I guess I didn't really want to believe people think like that anymore, let alone teach it to their kids."

Hilary rose to her feet and pulled a tissue from her pocket to blow her nose. "Thanks, DJ, you're a true friend. I just wish we could find a way to deal with Tony."

"You could tell Bridget and get him kicked out of here."

"Yes, I could do that."

"Or I could."

Hilary shook her head and stared up at the hills in Briones. "No . . . if anyone tells, it will be me."

That evening at Gran's, DJ told them what had happened. "Tony Andrada is creepo of the creepos. I don't blame Hilary for wanting to leave. Some plan Ames and I had—it didn't work at all. We've been ignoring him, but the only one he picks on is Hilary. And me, 'cause he knows I'm her friend."

"Changing someone's behavior can take a lot of time and effort." Joe set his paper down so he could see DJ.

"Our time is running out."

"You know, darlin', there's a Bible verse that says—"

"Gran, with you there's *always* a Bible verse!" DJ was getting exasperated.

Gran winked at her and continued. "This one fits perfectly. Jesus tells us to pray for our enemies, and so heap burning coals on their heads."

"Burning coals will work for Tony's head just fine. I'll help with the heaping."

"So, how about praying for him?"

"Gran, that's impossible. I can't do that."

"Would you pray for Tony if it could help Hilary? Keep her at the Academy?"

DJ stared at her grandmother. *Could* she pray for Tony? "I don't know."

"Then you need to pray another prayer first."

DJ sighed. "What's that?"

"A pastor friend of mine once told me that when you know you should do something and you can't, you should pray, 'Lord, make me willing to be willing.' Works every time."

"How about, 'Lord, make Tony willing'?" DJ shook her head at the look on her grandmother's face. "All right, I'll try." She sighed.

Gran shook her head.

"I'll do it, okay?" What had she gotten herself into this time?

13

THE PRAYERS WEREN'T WORKING.

"I'm sorry, DJ," Hilary said. "Even my dad said we should go somewhere else. We'll stay till the show and then I'm out of here."

"Oh, Hil, I don't want that to happen."

"Me neither, but we'll still be friends. I'll see you at shows and stuff."

"It won't be the same. I still think you should tell Bridget. She has a right to know."

"Dad says to write her a letter after I leave so it won't look like I'm asking her to make a choice. Besides, what can I say? 'Tony calls me names and such.' I should be tougher than that."

After the girls went about their work, DJ couldn't get Hilary's sad face out of her mind. *God, I thought you were going to work on this. I've been praying for Tony—sort of—and nothing's happening. Time's running out.*

She saddled Patches and prepared for a rough workout since he hadn't been on the lunge or hot walker. She needed the fight as much as he did.

Since it was the Tuesday before Thanksgiving and they were having company, Lindy had just finished making the bed in the spare room and setting out towels when DJ arrived at home. "Do you mind if the girls bunk down in your room? I thought they could choose between the family room, their parents' room, and yours. What do you think?"

"Whatever." It seemed strange that they were preparing to meet family for the first time. Robert's sister, Julia Gregory, her husband, Martin, and their two children were coming for Thanksgiving because Gran and Joe had invited everyone to their house for Thanksgiving dinner. The Gregorys lived in Connecticut and hadn't been able to come to the wedding.

"You've already stabled Bandit at Joe's so we can give the kids pony rides?"

"No, not till Friday. Joe and I thought we'd take everyone over to the Academy to look around. Mom, calm down. It isn't like the president of the United States is coming."

"Easy for you to say." Lindy stopped in the doorway with her hands on her hips. "At least it looks nice."

Looked nicer when Gran lived here. But DJ kept her thoughts to herself. She didn't want to shatter the truce that existed between her and her mother. Besides, Gran wasn't coming back, and DJ needed to live with that.

Lindy glanced at her watch. "Robert and our guests will be here any minute, so hurry up and change. Then we're going to Gran's for pizza."

"Mom, I already know all that. You've been over the weekend schedule sixty-five times." DJ ducked her mother's fake swing and headed for her room. Wouldn't it be nice if they could tease each other like this all the time?

Six-year-old Allison decided immediately that DJ belonged to her. She oohed and aahed over the pictures on DJ's bedroom walls and voted that her sleeping bag should definitely be spread in there.

Meredith, a year older than DJ at fifteen, looked bored with the entire thing. When she did take her earphones off, she acted as though she still had them on and ignored everyone. She chose to sleep in the family room—by herself.

When DJ entered Gran's house with Allison on one hand, Bobby and Billy wore matching thunderclouds on their faces. They glared at their cousins and parked right in front of DJ.

"Hi, guys. Do you remember Allison? You were still in diapers the last time you saw her." She nodded to each of the girls as she said the names. The twins eyed Allison suspiciously, as if sizing up the competition.

"I'm Bobby." The right twin pointed a thumb to his chest.

"I'm Billy, and DJ's our sister." They stepped forward, shoulder to shoulder.

"She likes us best."

DJ looked to Robert for help. All the adults were laughing and talking as if they'd forgotten all about the kids. Meredith had disappeared. If something didn't happen, they were going to have a war on their hands. Allison's lower lip stuck out as far as those on the twins.

"Hey, that's enough, I—"

"And we get to ride Bandit first." The Bs each grabbed one of DJ's legs and looked up. "Don't we?"

"No ponies for kids who don't share." Robert scooped a twin under each arm. "And that includes sharing DJ." He regarded his sons seriously until they each nodded and then put them down. "You guys show your cousin where the games are, or we can put a video on."

"Or I could read a story." DJ thanked Robert with her eyes.

"Or you could take a break," Robert said over his shoulder as he carried the twins into the other room.

"That's right," Julia said with a smile. "You are not the designated entertainment for the weekend or the baby-sitter. Come get something to drink and catch your breath."

"Thanks." DJ could tell she was going to like this relative. Julia gave you the feeling that she'd known you all her life and you were best friends. How'd she end up with a daughter like Meredith?

Andy and his wife, Sonya, along with their daughter Shawna, entered with armloads of pizza boxes. Andy was Joe's youngest son. Even nine-year-old Shawna carried a pizza box.

"Hi, all. Food's here." Andy led the way to the dining room and they spread the boxes out on the table.

"Everyone help yourself. The paper plates are over there," Gran pointed to a stack of wicker plate holders. "And the—"

"Drinks are in the kitchen," Joe finished for her. "Little kids get to eat at the breakfast table."

"DJ, come on!" One of the twins grabbed her hand and pulled.

"Nope, DJ is not one of the little kids. She can eat wherever she chooses." Robert saved the day again.

DJ took slices of the Hawaiian special and gourmet delight and wandered after the others into the family room. She sat down next to Andy and Sonya on the floor.

"So, how are the horses and riding coming?" Sonya asked around a mouthful of pizza.

"Good. Now that I have Major, it's even more fun." DJ took a bite of the topping-heavy pizza cradled in her hand. "You playing much volleyball?"

The conversation swirled around her with everyone

laughing, talking, and teasing one another as if they'd been together the weekend before. It would have been easy to feel left out, but Andy made sure she was part of the conversation. When the twins charged back in, Sonya grabbed them and wrestled them to the floor.

"Run, DJ. Run for your life!"

DJ ran, but only as far as the dining room for more pizza. She was just scooping a slice onto her plate when she heard someone ask, "So, Robert, when's the wedding?"

DJ froze in midaction. She looked up just in time to see Robert flinch.

"I . . . ah . . . we haven't set a date yet."

DJ glanced at her mother. She wore a smile that almost disguised her tight jaw. But DJ knew her mother too well. Lindy didn't like being pressured.

"We decided we needed to get to know each other better before marriage." Lindy's words were true, but DJ wasn't fooled.

"DJ, we was missing you." The twins glommed to her like magnets. DJ sighed and smiled down at them. "Where is Allison?" She didn't bother asking about Meredith. That cousin had made it clear she had no time for people who rode horses.

"Watching *The Little Mermaid*. Can you give us horsey rides?"

"No, she can't, but I can." Andy grabbed the gigglers up and dropped to the floor. Both boys climbed onto his back and away they went. Hearing the laughter, Allison clamored for a turn. Within minutes the Bs were riding Robert and Joe while Andy carried Allison. The "horses" raced down the hall on hands and knees. The riders shouted "giddy-up," the men cried, "outta my way," and the women laughed till the tears came.

In bed that night, DJ caught herself giggling again at the thought of the inside race. Allison was already sound asleep after her telling of "The Three Bears," complete with voices to suit the characters. DJ crossed her arms over her stomach. What a crazy evening. Even if Robert didn't marry her mother, they were still a part of this wacko family. *Bet Grandpa Joe's knees hurt tomorrow.*

That was the first thing she asked when he stopped by for her in the morning.

"Oh, some. But I beat out Robert and Andy. Not bad for an old guy." Gray fog had lightened as they fed the horses and cleaned the stalls.

The chill made DJ shiver.

"You should have worn a jacket, child." Joe tossed out the last of the dirty shavings.

"It'll burn off. If shoveling this stuff doesn't warm you up, what will?"

"You recovered from all the attention last night?"

"You mean the kids?" DJ leaned on the handle of her fork. "I wasn't the one giving horseback rides."

"To be honest, someone should have shot me and put me out of my misery. My kneecaps!" He shook his head with a laugh.

They were both laughing when they saddled up and headed for the arena.

"Hi, Tony." Joe lifted a hand in greeting.

DJ shot her grandfather a startled look.

"Hi, Joe." Tony reigned his horse to ride on Joe's other side. "How's the cutting-horse training coming along?" He didn't say anything to DJ, and she squeezed Major into a trot.

She didn't hear Joe's answer. She didn't want to. Here they'd been having a perfectly good time together and that . . . that—no, she wouldn't ruin Thanksgiving Day by calling anyone names.

DJ worked Major on the flat until a sweat rose on his shoulders, then the pair transferred out to the jumping arena. *Concentrate,* she ordered herself over and over.

Following Bridget's advice, DJ tried to keep her self-talk positive. That way, she couldn't think of Tony—or Hilary or anything besides jumping. She stayed with the low jumps, focusing on her posture, her hands, and, as always, her head and eyes.

Major lifted off as if he were floating, each jump effortless as they moved in perfect sync. The sun peeked through, melting away the remaining fog. Around they went, back across the ring and over the jumps.

DJ heard another rider enter the arena. She looked up. Tony!

"Guess that's enough, fella." She put Major to the final jump. He pulled to the right and ticked the pole. The words she muttered to herself were not positive as they rode back to the barn.

After cooling Major out and putting him away, she bridled and mounted Bandit to ride him to Gran's. You'd have thought she brought Santa Claus the way the little kids greeted her.

"Okay, I get breakfast before anyone rides. That's the rule." She tied the pony to the fence with his lead shank, removed the bridle and saddle, and headed for the back door.

The smell of roasting turkey wafted through the house. DJ sniffed and closed her eyes to better appreciate the fragrance. How come turkey smelled best on Thanksgiving? She followed the sounds of laughter into the kitchen, where most of the family was gathered, either drinking coffee at the table or preparing food at the counters.

"Good morning, darlin'." Gran turned from the dough she was kneading to give DJ a kiss.

"Homemade rolls?" DJ snitched a bit of dough. "Anything for breakfast for a starving granddaughter?"

Orange juice, a cinnamon roll, and a bowl of mixed fresh fruit appeared on the table at the same time she sat down.

"You want some hot chocolate, too?" Julia asked. "The other kids sure enjoyed it."

DJ nodded around a mouthful of cinnamon roll.

"Maybe she'd rather have coffee. She's almost an adult now," Andy added.

"No thanks, hot chocolate will be fine. But you could put a drop of coffee into it."

"Ah, we have a mocha lover here." Martin leaned forward. "I knew it yesterday when we met—a girl after my own heart."

DJ grinned back and kept on eating. Each of the Bs had already been in the house asking when she would be ready.

"Where's Mom?" She looked at Gran. "And Robert?"

"They're over looking at the new house." Gran winked. "I think they wanted to be alone."

Uh-oh, that might not be too good. DJ sipped her hot mocha. She could feel the warmth circle around her belly. Was Lindy over her grump of the night before?

By the time DJ had given each kid three rides, settled forty-two arguments, refereed thirteen fights, and heard "DJ" one thousand times, she was ready to turn in her cousin badge.

What she really wanted to do was eat dinner in the garage, on the condition that no one under five feet follow her. Maybe Meredith was the smarter of the two, always disappearing.

"No, DJ and Meredith are eating with the grown-ups. They'll be in here just for grace," Joe settled firmly. "Andy and Sonya are hosting this table." He parked the twins on phone books so they could see better. "Now we're all going to say grace together."

He took a hand of each twin and raised his voice. "Okay, everyone! God is great, God is good, and we thank Him for our food. Amen."

DJ headed to the dining room with a sigh of relief. The kids were fun, but oh, she was ready for some peace and quiet.

By the time everyone had eaten their fill, the kids were ready to ride again.

Robert shook his head. "No, DJ is off limits. You can watch a video or play a game or go play outside, but no pony and no DJ."

DJ sent him a silent thanks and went to find Joe. They needed to go feed Major and Ranger, and she needed some peace and quiet. Her ears were still ringing from the kids' endlessly calling her name.

By the time Sunday evening rolled around, DJ enjoyed the quiet of her own house. She'd been sad to see the Gregorys, except Meredith, leave for Connecticut and had really had a fabulous time like everyone else. Everyone, that is, but her mother. DJ could tell something was bothering her mom. The twins were still at Gran's, and Robert and Lindy were off someplace together.

DJ flipped the channels on the television until she found a mystery movie and settled in to watch. She'd already finished her homework, and with the bowl of popcorn on her lap, she didn't have to get up for anyone or anything.

A car pulled into the driveway.

"I don't think so," her mother said in the doorway. "Good night, Robert."

DJ flinched. She knew that tone well. She huddled deep into the security of the wing chair, wishing she were up in her room and sound asleep in bed. Her mother entered the room.

"I suppose you'd like to know that I told Robert I wouldn't marry him. I know that's what you wanted. Now you can finally be happy." With that, Lindy marched up the stairs, down the hall, and slammed her bedroom door.

DJ started to get to her feet, but the shock of the news pushed her back. "Fiddle. Double and triple fiddle."

"NO SCHOOL TOMORROW. What do you want to do?"

"We should spend the day getting ready for the show." Always practical Amy.

"How about taking a lunch and heading up into Briones? We don't have to stay too long." DJ closed her eyes. "Just think—trees, trails, hills. I'm so tired of flat arenas I could croak."

"Right." Amy shook her head. "The day DJ Randall turns down a chance to ride just because the ground is flat is—"

"You know what I mean. Come on, Ames, we'll work extra fast and then go. We can give the horses baths when we get back." DJ rested one foot on the curb to prop up her bike. She sent Amy a pleading look. "You don't want me to go without you, do you?"

"I'll ask and call you. Mom's got the Cub Scouts here right now." Amy waved and pushed her bike into the cluttered garage. With four kids, there were always toys and sports gear, school books, and other stuff lying around.

DJ walked into an empty house. As usual, she answered the blinking light to find out where her mother was. "I'm going to dinner with Robert. We won't be late."

DJ shook her head. You had to give the man an *A* for

persistence. Even after Mom said she wouldn't marry him, he kept coming around. They'd been on the phone every night, and he'd come to visit on Tuesday.

DJ thought about the wedding that wasn't going to be while she heated some leftover soup and made a sandwich. Her plan had been to keep Robert and her mother apart. Well, they weren't apart, but the wedding was off. And her plan had nothing to do with it, even though it was obvious her mother halfway blamed DJ. But now DJ found herself rooting for Robert.

What would life be like with the Bs around all the time? Noisy, but they could learn to stay out of her room when she needed some space. What about Robert?

She took her tray into the family room and settled into the wing chair. He wasn't too bossy. Actually, he was a pretty nice guy. And rich. Well, not really, but he sure had more money than she'd ever seen in her life. And he said he'd help her go for her Olympic dream. Was that the only reason she now thought the marriage might be a good thing?

That would be really creepy of her. One thing was sure: She wouldn't come home to an empty house anymore. He'd even said he'd keep the nanny so Mom could continue her career.

DJ swung one foot and tucked the other underneath her. Robert was right—this house wasn't big enough for that many people.

She shrugged and turned on the television. What did any of this matter now? Her mother had decided against the wedding.

But that night in her prayers, DJ changed her request. "God, my plan sure doesn't seem to be a good idea anymore. Now that Mom and Robert aren't getting married, I don't like it." She stopped to think. "Gran always says we should ask for what we want and then thank you for doing what's best. Is that what's going on here, or did I mess up big time?" She waited, hoping for an answer.

She heard Lindy come up the stairs. Was her mother crying?

It wouldn't be the first time this week.

DJ tried to return to her prayer. "So, do you have a plan that's better than mine?" She could still hear sobs.

She threw back the covers with a sigh. Her mother's bedroom door was closed. Obviously she didn't want any company. DJ turned back toward her room, then with a shrug, tapped on the bedroom door. All Mom could do was yell at her or tell her to go away. So what?

"Yes."

"Can I come in?" When there was no answer, DJ pushed open the door just a crack and peeked in. Lindy sat on the edge of the bed blowing her nose and looking as if she'd been crying for hours. Red eyes, mussed hair, and a mound of crumpled tissues on the bed gave her away.

"Can I get you something?" DJ paused in front of her mom. "How about some tea or hot chocolate?"

"That would be nice." Lindy sighed and wiped her eyes. "I don't know what's come over me. All I do is cry lately." She rubbed the spot where the diamond engagement ring had been, then flopped back on the bed, one hand on her forehead.

"I'll be right back." DJ clattered down the stairs and set the teakettle to heating. She took out a box of tea bags and one of cocoa packets and got out two mugs. By the time she had the tray set, the teapot shrilled. She fixed the hot chocolate, topped it with miniature marshmallows, and carried the tray back upstairs.

What could she say? If only Gran were here. She always had the perfect words.

Lindy had changed into a pair of silk pajamas and folded back the covers of the bed. The tissue pile had disappeared, but the box sat on top of the nightstand, within easy reach.

"DJ, I don't know what I did right to deserve as good a kid as you." Lindy accepted the steaming mug with a nod of thanks. "I sure haven't been the kind of mother who helped make you that way, that's for certain." She set the mug down and swung her bare feet up onto the bed. Scooting toward the middle, she patted the edge for DJ to sit down.

"That's okay, you were busy. I had Gran." DJ sipped after blowing on the hot liquid. The screen-saver images on the computer flashed different colored patterns in the corner. Outside, a dog barked.

"DJ, I'm just so scared." The words sounded small in the stillness.

"Scared? You? Hey, you're not afraid of anything." With one leg up on the bed, DJ turned so she could see her mother better.

Lindy pushed her hair back with a shaking hand. "Yes, I am. The thought of marriage makes my stomach hurt. And look what kind of a mother I am. I yell at you or don't talk to you. I expect you to be the adult around here when you're just a kid. You shouldn't have to bring me hot chocolate and listen to me cry." She snorted. "That's my job."

"Well, I'm not the one who's sad right now. You can do this for me when it's my turn." DJ watched as another tear brimmed over and ran down her mother's face. If only she dared reach over and wipe it away. Instead, she handed her mother a tissue.

"See what I mean." Lindy took it and wiped before the next one could fall. "A waterworks, that's what I am." She tossed the tissue toward the wastebasket, but it missed and floated to the floor. "I've even prayed about this. I pleaded with God to tell me what to do, but there's been no answer.

I know Gran gets answers all the time. She must have an inside track or something."

"She's been praying for you."

"Oh, I'm sure she has. Robert has, too—look where it's gotten him."

"Gran says God can't guide you unless you're already moving."

"What's that supposed to mean?"

"I don't really know—it just came to mind." DJ wished she knew what to say. *God, please help me.*

"So what do you think? Should we marry Robert?"

"We?" DJ's voice squeaked on the words. "*I'm* not the one getting married."

"No, but you're my family." Lindy reached over and patted DJ's knee. "I know how you feel. You've made your opinion abundantly clear. Don't worry, DJ, love isn't fatal. I'll get over it." Her voice cracked on the words.

"But, Mom . . ."

"Good night, dear, and thank you for the comfort."

"Good night." DJ picked up the tray and left. How *did* she feel? She wasn't sure anymore.

"What can I do, God?" she asked later just before falling asleep. "We have to come up with a new plan." Or had her plan been the reason everything was so messed up? Scary thought.

DJ woke in the night to the sound of her mother's crying again.

"How about if we ask Joe to go with us?" DJ gave her saddle one last swipe with the polish rag.

"Fine with me." Amy held up her headstall. All the conches shone in the sunlight. "But my mom said I have to be home by five."

DJ leaped to her feet. "Then we better get out of here." She trotted through the barn and out to the stalls where Joe was brushing down Ranger. "You want to ride up in Briones with Amy and me?"

"Sure, when?"

"Now. I'll even share my lunch." DJ gave Ranger a rub on his nose. Major nickered in the next stall. "Come on, guy, let's get saddled." She led the big horse out and tied him in front of the tack room. By the time she'd answered fifteen questions from her students, found a missing brush, and finished saddling Major, twenty minutes had passed.

Amy met her at the gate. "Where's Joe?"

"Coming. If I don't get out of here, the munchkins will snag me again. They're so jealous about our trail ride, they're turning green." DJ opened the gate. "Let's wait up the trail a bit."

Just then Joe rode up, followed by Tony Andrada. "Hope it's okay. I asked Tony if he'd like to come along."

DJ stared at Joe. What could she say? Tony Andrada, the creep of all creeps. What a way to ruin a so-far perfect day.

"Fine, why not?" She could tell from the look on Tony's face that he understood her sarcastic comment. He didn't look as if he wanted to be with them either.

DJ and Amy trotted their horses up the tree-shaded trail. Off to the right snaked a gully that ran with water during the winter. Squirrels scolded the riders for invading their territory, and scrub jays squawked their own brand of insults. When they could ride side by side, DJ and Amy hung on to the lead. Single file, DJ went ahead. She didn't want to be any closer to Tony than she had to, and right now she wasn't at all happy with her grandfather. The nerve of Joe, inviting Creepo along. He knew how she felt about the guy.

The ride wasn't nearly as much fun as she'd thought it

would be. It was all Tony's fault.

Once they reached the open meadows, she nudged Major into a canter. "Come on, Ames, let's go." The two galloped along the fire road that curved around the meadow and up to the Briones Crest Trail. Sunlight, blue sky, even a puffy cloud or two. The day was definitely improving. Horse hooves pounded the packed dirt road, a steer bellowing at their interruption. DJ laughed—without Tony, it would have been perfect.

At a shout behind them, DJ turned in the saddle to see Tony galloping across the meadow. He was not keeping to the fire road.

"Oh, fiddle. That stupid—" Before she could finish her sentence, Tony's horse stumbled. Tony yelled and flew through the air, landing crumpled on the ground.

Horrified, DJ reigned Major around, and she and Amy pelted back to the fallen boy. Joe rode up at the same moment, dismounting in a fluid motion and throwing the reins to DJ.

At the look on his face, DJ shook her head. "It's not my fault. I never thought Tony was stupid enough to ride through the gopher holes."

The sternness in Joe's eyes silenced her.

He thought it was her fault.

Tony hadn't moved. His horse stood, head hanging, one hoof barely touching the ground.

God, please don't let him be really hurt. I'm sorry. Please.

DJ and Amy dismounted, keeping their gaze on Joe, who was examining Tony for broken bones.

Tony groaned. "I . . . I can't breathe." A whisper. He raised his head. "My horse?"

"Do you hurt anywhere?" Joe rested back on his heels, his hands gentle as they unbuckled the boy's helmet.

"Everywhere." He wiggled his hands and feet. "But I'm not broken anywhere." With Joe's assistance, he sat up.

When he held up his head, the bruise that was fast turning purple shone bright. He lifted a hand to touch it and flinched.

"Are you dizzy? Feel like throwing up? Sharp pain anywhere?"

Tony shook his head at the questions. "Just got knocked out, that's all. Y'all needn't worry about me." He looked up at Amy. "Thanks for catching my horse."

"He didn't run off. His leg is hurt too bad."

DJ hunkered down and inspected the already swelling foreleg. "I don't think it's broken, just sprained. He can put his weight on it but is limping pretty bad."

Tony let Joe help him to his feet. At the first step, he nearly fell. "Ow!" He grabbed his leg. "Talk about sprains." He pressed against the side of his boot.

"Don't take it off—the boot will help keep the swelling down."

"Should we go tell Bridget to bring up the van?" Amy asked Joe. "If fire trucks can make it up here, she can, too."

"Let's give it a moment and see how both Tony and the horse feel." Joe turned to his saddlebags. "I brought cans of soda for everyone. Tony, you sit there and prop your foot on that rock. DJ, Amy—you brought food, right?"

Joe still hadn't looked at DJ. She felt like spraining her leg just so he would look at her with all the concern he was wasting on the creepo. And now she was supposed to share her lunch. Could things get much worse?

They could. After the food was gone, Joe helped Tony to his feet again. "Well, you can't walk your horse out, that's for sure. How about if I lead him?" He turned to look at DJ. "DJ, Major can ride double."

"Tony can ride Josh. I don't mind walking." Amy stepped forward.

"No, thanks for volunteering. DJ?"

"All right." Why should she have to give Tony a ride—

the fall was his fault. He'd ruined their whole day. "Get on," she hissed, her back to Joe so he couldn't see her.

"I'd rather walk."

"Well, I'd rather you walked, too, but when Joe says to do something, it's best to do it." She stabbed a finger in his direction. "Now, get on."

Once Tony was mounted, DJ accepted Joe's assistance to get in the saddle. Still, he said nothing more to her. She felt like giving the rider behind her an elbow in the gut.

"You're the biggest snob I ever knew." He made sure his whisper didn't carry to Joe's ears.

"Redneck."

"How would you know?"

"I heard the way you talk to Hilary. She's gone out of her way to help you, and you keep on making her life miserable. If she wasn't so nice, she'd have told Bridget about you weeks ago, and you'da been out on your can."

"I suppose you're one of those do-gooder Christians." The tone of his voice said what he thought of those who followed Christ.

"Sure am. So's Hilary—that's why she puts up with you."

"You okay back there?" Joe called from the front of the line.

"Fine, sir," Tony answered.

"You may be fine, but I'm sure not. I'd rather dump you in the creek."

"Just let me off, Miss Christian. I can walk."

DJ nudged Major into a trot.

Tony groaned and hung on for all his worth.

In a few steps, DJ ordered Major to walk again. Where had she gotten such a mean streak? Was this the way Jesus wanted her to act? What would Gran say if she knew what was happening? Joe knew, and that meant Gran would hear about it.

They were halfway down the trail when Tony asked, "So why hasn't Hilary told Bridget?"

"Because Bridget wants us to learn to handle things on our own. Each student worker is assigned a new person to train. You got Hilary, the best trainer of all." DJ wanted to add, *And if you don't knock off the racial slurs, Hilary will leave,* but she'd promised not to say anything. "You're lucky—you really are."

Hilary was the first to see them ride back onto the Academy grounds. She ran up the hill and took the reins of the injured horse. "What happened?" She looked up to see Tony behind DJ. "Are you hurt?"

"Take his horse to the stall and get some ice while we unsaddle these horses. DJ can ride Tony over to the office. When will your mother be here, son?"

"Six."

"Then we better call her. You probably should get that ankle looked at." Joe dismounted at the barn door. "Go on, DJ, take him over while I put Ranger away."

DJ did as he said. How could Hilary take care of Tony's horse like that when he'd been so mean to her? Let alone be polite to him?

In front of the office, DJ slung her leg over Major's neck and slid to the ground. "If you scoot up the saddle . . . no, that won't work." She stepped closer to the horse. "If you slide off carefully, I can catch you so you don't put all your weight on that foot." Between them, they got Tony sitting on one of the chunks of log kept there for that purpose.

"If you'll hold Major's reins, I'll go call your mom." DJ got his phone number and dialed. After telling his mother what happened, she returned to the shady spot where Tony now had his injured leg propped on another wood block. "She'll be here as soon as she can. You want me to get you some ice while we wait?"

Tony looked up at her as though he didn't trust what he

was hearing. "Y'all sure you want to do that?"

"Yes or no."

"Yes, please."

DJ returned with two plastic bags filled with ice cubes. She helped stack them around the ankle of his dusty boot. "Sorry you won't be in the show tomorrow."

"Me too." He stared at the ice bags. "Thanks for the ride."

"You're welcome." DJ headed back to the barn, Major trotting behind her. Joe and Hilary were working with the injured horse, and Amy was brushing Ranger and Josh down. DJ put her tack away. "You ready to wash?"

Together, they bathed their horses, brushed them, and fastened on coolers. By the time they were finished, Amy dashed for her bike to head home. "See you in the morning," she called over her shoulder.

DJ fed both Ranger and Major before ambling back to the stall where Joe had just finished. "He going to be all right?"

"With some rest. Lucky he didn't break it."

"Joe, I'm sorry." DJ looked up at him. "Please don't hate me."

"Hate you?" Joe shook his head and laid a hand on her shoulder. "Never. I was disappointed in you, though. Riding off like that was thoughtless."

"But everyone knows to stay on the trails. You'd think . . ." She stopped. The thought that they might have had to destroy Tony's horse made her heart pound. If that had happened, she never would have forgiven herself. If today had been part of God's plan for answering her prayers, she sure didn't understand Him.

"I better get home. Show mornings always come earlier than others." At the thought, her butterflies took a practice flight. After a day like today, who knew what tomorrow would bring?

15

SHOW TIME—TWO DAYS' WORTH.

"This is our day, big guy. I can feel it." DJ tickled Major's upper lip, loving the whiskery feel on her fingertips. She could hear the sounds of other riders readying their horses for transport. Horses nickered, and a whinny came from off to the right, floating through the fog like a phantom song.

DJ shivered in the chill. One good thing about summer shows, she didn't freeze getting to the site. But then, today, even after the sun came out, she wouldn't be sweating bullets, either. She forked out the dirty shavings while Major ate his breakfast, then brought up a cart of clean bedding to dump in as soon as he was out of the stall. That way, he wouldn't get more dust on him.

DJ picked his hooves. She probably should have had him shod first, but it was too late now. She always put it off as long as she could because it made such a dent in her bank account. At this rate, she'd never get a new saddle.

"Mornin', kid," Joe said with a grin.

"Overslept, did you?" DJ dropped the last hoof.

"Now, none of your smart remarks. I'm supposed to be retired, you know."

"Plain tired's more like it." DJ hid a snicker. Giving Joe

a bad time was almost as much fun as teasing Gran. "By the way, I fed your starving horse for you. *He* shouldn't suffer because you can't get out from under the covers." It wasn't as if Joe didn't feed Major every morning, but laughing at the menacing look on his face made her feel lighter and less nervous.

She jogged past the other riders to find Bridget.

"We will send the jumpers first load, as usual," Bridget said, consulting her clipboard. "Mr. Yamamoto is in charge. By the way, DJ, Tony called to say he would not be showing today but that his ankle is only sprained. They had the vet out to check on his horse, and he will be out of commission for a couple of weeks. What happened up there?"

DJ's first racing thought was *Tony didn't tell her*. The second: *Please don't ask me any more questions about it*. "Ah . . . Tony's horse tripped and threw him." That much was the truth.

"Were you racing?"

DJ stared at Bridget as if she'd left some of her marbles at home. "No way!" A swift knife stab of pain that Bridget would even think that, and another of guilt. Technically, it could have been called racing by an innocent bystander.

"Well, then, I am glad no one was injured worse. It is a shame that Tony has to miss the last big show of the season."

"Yeah, right." DJ headed for the trailer. *I'm sure we'll all miss him terribly*.

DJ trotted over to where the slight man wearing the Academy sweat shirt was letting down the ramp to the six-horse trailer. "Who you want first, Dad?" Mr. Yamamoto told all the student workers to call him Dad—he claimed it made life easier.

"If Major is ready, let's start with him, then Prince. Have you seen Hilary yet?"

DJ shook her head. "I'll go see if he's been fed. Maybe

something happened to make her late."

With a swift dash by Prince's stall to see that he was eating, DJ told Amy to get a move on readying Major. The barns were bustling as she dodged horses, kids, adults, and a baby in a stroller. Life at the Academy was definitely a family affair.

"Major's first." DJ slipped under the tie across her stall opening and snapped the lead shank to her horse's halter.

"I'll throw those shavings in as soon as you get going." Joe checked the buckles on the sheet and gave Major an extra pat. "You're out of here, kid."

"Thanks." DJ swallowed her resident troupe of butterflies and clucked to Major. Was there any more exciting place on earth than a barn preparing for a show? Her broad grin brought forth answering smiles and greetings from everyone she met.

Major walked into the trailer as if he did it every weekday and three times on Sunday. Josh followed while DJ went to get Prince. That was the rule: If riders weren't there to take care of their horses, whoever was would do it for them.

She stopped by Tony's stall to see the gelding. The horse turned from his grain pan and nickered. "At least *you* know how to be polite." DJ looked around to make sure no one else heard her.

She opened the web gate to Prince's stall and snapped a lead shank to his halter. "Hey, guy, come with me, okay?" The rangy Thoroughbred snuffled her shoulder and followed docilely.

If DJ let herself think ahead to the show-ring, she wouldn't be able to keep her feet on the hard-packed dirt.

But where was Hilary?

For the first time in DJ's memory, the horses were loaded with no fireworks on the loading ramp. Even Patches walked right in as if he'd been doing this all his life.

Mrs. Johnson clapped her hands like a little kid. DJ's students wore grins that nearly chased the sleep from their eyes. But still no Hilary.

"You want me to call her?" DJ asked Bridget.

"If you want." She handed DJ a slip of paper. "Here's her number."

DJ let the phone ring and ring. No answer. "They must be on the way."

"Maybe she slept through her alarm," suggested Krissie from her place glued to DJ's right hip. The little blonde had been bouncing like a tennis ball all morning.

DJ shook her head. "Not Hilary. The show means too much to her." DJ felt a little worm of fear wriggle in her belly. *Please, God, don't let anything have happened to Hilary*.

They loaded students into the vans and cars with their waiting parents, and the caravan eased out of the drive. DJ rode in the front seat of Joe's Explorer. Last time Tony had been riding in that spot—and Hilary had been in back with her. Things sure were different today. DJ didn't like it one bit.

"Gran will be coming with Lindy, and Robert will meet them there with the boys." Joe looked over at her with a smile.

DJ groaned. "Now you tell me. Do they have to come?"

"Why, child, I thought you'd be pleased."

"I am—I think. But when my family's around, the butterflies act as if I'm performing for the president of the Olympic games or something. Joe, you have no idea what I feel like inside."

"Sure I do. When I was a member of the force's mounted drill team, I had worse butterflies than when I faced an angry crowd. The anticipation gets to you."

Even after they had the horses tied to the rope stretched between trees and the announcer had made the first call for Hunter/Jumper, Hilary wasn't there.

"Should we saddle her horse?" DJ and Amy looked at each other.

"Yeah, she'll be here." Amy turned to leave. "You saddle Prince, and I'll go ask Bridget to make sure Hilary is last on the program."

"Good idea." DJ had already changed into her riding gear, but, with Joe's help, she managed to stay neat.

God, please, please, please *make Hilary all right. Help her to get here in time.* The prayer kept pace with her hands as she brushed the tall sorrel horse. Hilary usually braided Prince's mane—DJ should have done that.

She looked over at Major. She and Joe had finished his braid just a few minutes before. The red ribbons made Major look like a professional show horse. Having someone to help her sure made a difference. A nice difference. What would it be like when the boys and Shawna started showing? The thought made her gasp. What a circus that would be!

"DJ, we's here."

"Good luck, DJ. Now stay back, boys. You can hug DJ later." Robert grinned at her. "We just wanted you to know you had a rooting section."

"You look pretty, DJ. Major too." The boys couldn't move. Robert had them in a steel grip.

"Say goodbye. See you later."

As they left, the squawk boxes announced the second call for Hunter/Jumper.

DJ mounted Major, and Joe unsnapped Prince's lead line. Together, they started around the track to the warm-up ring on the other side of the huge covered arena. The Black Diamond Riding Center sprawled over ten acres and looked like a place out of the movies. Tubs of blooming plants, white-board fences, a shaded picnic area, and an enclosed plot with swings and climbing equipment for bored children. With stalls for over a hundred horses and four rings beside the covered area, the place made DJ drool.

But where was Hilary?

Riders loosening up their horses circled the open arena, big enough to equal the two at Briones combined.

"Hilary's on last. You're in the middle," Amy said with a rush. "How about if I warm up Prince?"

"Good idea." Together, the two girls entered the arena and joined the circling throng. If all of these riders were entered in Hunter/Jumper, the class would take hours. DJ's heart sank. She didn't have a chance.

She put that thought out of her mind and focused on Major, slowly warming him up and concentrating on the event ahead of them.

The announcer called the first entrant. She could hear the applause and then a groan from the spectators.

The next time around the arena she saw Joe flag Amy. Hilary stood by his side. DJ trotted over to join them. "What happened?"

"First our car wouldn't start, then it stalled halfway here." Hilary adjusted her stirrups and mounted as she spoke. "I can't thank you enough for taking care of Prince for me." She held out a hand. "See, I can't quit shaking."

"Take a deep breath and let it all out." Bridget had joined them. "You will be fine. Relax your shoulders and breath deeply again." Bridget's voice held all the calm of a summer lake. "Now, Hilary, you know how to concentrate, so get out there and do it. Forget what has happened and do your job."

"Thanks, Bridget. How is Tony's horse?"

"He will be okay in a week or two. Thank you for all the extra time you put in with him last night."

DJ looked from Hilary to Amy and gave a brief shake of her head. What was Hilary, a saint or something? Amy raised an eyebrow. It was obvious she wondered the same.

"Two more and you're on." Bridget nodded toward the gate to the show-ring. "Do your best. That's all anyone can ask."

DJ waited her turn, Joe standing beside her.

"I think it's worse being your grandfather than showing myself." He looked up at DJ with a smile. "Know what I mean?"

"Yep, that's how I feel when my students are in the ring. I want them to do well so badly." DJ stroked Major's neck. "You know, nothing seems to bother this guy. He's calm as a sleeping dog, but I can tell he's ready to go."

"His years of police training in action. Sure wish it worked for me." He wiped a bead of sweat from his forehead. "Okay, kid, do it. I'm going up into the stands where I can see better."

The announcer called DJ's number. She took a deep breath, let it out, and trotted into the ring.

"Go, DJ! Y'all can do it."

The Southern accent. She didn't dare look. Tony Andrada was in the stands and cheering for *her*.

DJ put everything out of her mind but the jumps ahead. She signaled Major and away they went. Plain fences, an oxer, three jumps of varying heights, an in and out, a brush. DJ thrilled to being airborne. She and Major were one. The rhythm of canter, thrust, fly, and land echoed in her heart. Perfect. Yes! This was what she wanted most in life.

They completed the round to a burst of applause. Two small voices screamed, "DJ! DJ!" A glance up at the stand told her the entire family was there, even Andy and Sonya with Shawna.

DJ bit her lip. They had *all* come to see her and Major. She rode out of the ring to their enthusiastic cheers.

"Way to go." Tony, on crutches, was the last to congratulate her.

"That was some jumping, kid, and, Major, you didn't look too bad yourself." Joe met her outside. He clapped one hand on DJ's knee and slapped the horse's shoulder with the other. "I'm so proud of you I could pop."

Amy trotted up. "That was great, DJ. And did you notice who is here?"

"I know. Tony. I can't believe it."

"And he was cheering for you—man, was he ever cheering. What do you think happened?"

"Got me." She stopped to listen. "Hilary's up next. I want to go watch."

"I'll take Major, you go on." Joe reached for the reins. "I already saw the jumper most important to me."

DJ blew him a kiss as she dismounted and ran for the arena.

Hilary jumped a flawless routine.

Tony Andrada shouted and cheered as if they were best friends.

"God must've done a miracle." DJ looked at Amy and shook her head. "I can't believe it."

Five people made it into the second round, DJ and Hilary included.

"I thought last time was bad—this is worse." Even under her gloves, a hangnail tempted DJ to chew it. She wouldn't make it around the arena again. She had to go to the bathroom.

The first entrant knocked a bar down. The second jumped clean.

DJ rode in third position. "Okay, fella, this is the test." With each clean jump, she felt more like she was flying. Up, airborne, and down. Major kept his ears forward and grunted with each landing. "One more." Thrust, fly, and—the tick echoed in her mind. She finished the course and exited to cheers, Tony one of the loudest.

DJ glanced up at her cheering sections—one made up

of family, the other of academy riders.

The fourth entry's horse refused a jump. That left only Hilary.

Joe again held Major so DJ could watch. She stood with her hands behind her back, fingers crossed and prayers flying heavenward. Amy, right beside her, did the same.

Hilary and Prince jumped a clean round to the roar of the spectators. She'd have to go another. While the attendants raised the poles another two inches, DJ dashed outside.

"Don't worry, I'll stay here." Joe waved her back to the arena.

DJ felt as though she'd chew all her fingernails down to the quick. But with her fingers locked in a prayer, that would have been hard.

The first entry, a man, trotted into the ring. But, with a perfect round, he rushed the last jump. The pole wobbled and fell.

"Come on, Hilary. Even a tick will take it now. Do it, Hil, do it."

Hilary Jones jumped a perfect round.

DJ and Amy stamped their feet, pounded their hands together, and screamed at the top of their lungs.

"You've got to get your ribbon." Amy jabbed her friend with her elbow.

"Oh, right." DJ flew back out to mount Major. She followed the others back into the ring and accepted the third-place white ribbon. This time she didn't feel badly about not placing higher. A white ribbon in a group this size was fantastic.

When she stopped Major in front of Joe, she grinned at him. "Thanks for the horse, GJ."

"You're welcome." He let out a sigh as if he'd been swimming under water. "Let's go put this animal away, and I'll treat you to—I don't know, whatever they have over at that food room that looks good. I feel like I've been jumping those hurdles myself."

"DJ, I can't thank you and Amy enough. I'd have had to cancel without you." Hilary stopped her horse on the edge of the group.

"No problem. You'd have done the same for us."

"You did the same for me." Tony leaned on his crutches. "Bridget told me how you worked with my horse last night."

"It was nothing. That's the way we do things at Briones."

"Yeah, well . . . thanks."

DJ watched him hobble back to the arena. She shook her head. "Can you beat that?"

That afternoon after lunch, DJ took a breather from her showing and teaching duties. She joined her family in the stands and propped her elbows on the bench seat behind her.

"Want a cookie, darlin'?" Gran leaned over Joe to offer DJ a chocolate chip cookie.

"Yes, thank you." Joe took it and bit into it.

"Not you, you big galoot." Gran thumped him on the arm.

"You said darlin'." He winked at DJ and looked soulfully at Gran. "How was I to know which darlin' you meant?"

Gran dug in her box for another cookie. She shook her head at the clamoring Bs and handed it to DJ. "You'd think these characters hadn't already eaten half the box."

"Thanks, Gran." DJ munched and watched as Gran opened the box and let the boys each have another cookie. "You're a soft touch." She looked at Shawna sitting quietly on her other side. "Did you get any?"

The girl nodded. "DJ, you were awesome. You think I'll be able to ride like that someday?"

Andy groaned. "Next I suppose we'll have to buy a house out here, too."

"Really, Daddy?" Shawna's blue eyes lit up as if someone had just turned on a Christmas tree. "When?"

"We'll just send her to live with Robert and the boys." Sonya reached over Gran's shoulder and helped herself to a cookie. "How's your house coming?"

"Plans are finalized, now I just need approval from Contra Costa County. As soon as the permits are in my hand, my men'll go to work." Robert stretched his long legs over the seat in front of him. "Boys, no running." He snagged one of the Bs by the back of his shirt.

"Hey, Lindy, did you get approval for your thesis?" Sonya turned to ask.

"Probably Monday. It looks pretty safe."

DJ glanced at her mother. How come she hadn't told her daughter? You'd think that was good enough news to share. But DJ remembered back to the scene in the bedroom the night before. Probably her mother hadn't been thinking much about her thesis when she was crying over Robert. Grown-ups were so strange.

A shriek, cut off by a thud, derailed the thought. DJ leaped to her feet. But not before Lindy, who was closest to the edge of the bleachers. She was over the side and on the floor before anyone could blink.

By the time DJ got there, Lindy had the twin who'd taken a header off the bleachers cuddled in her arms, a gentle hand smoothing back hair already slick with blood.

"There now," she murmured, rocking him at the same time. "You'll be okay."

When Robert tried to take Bobby into his own arms, the little guy clung to Lindy.

Joe put a folded handkerchief on the streaming cut and

held it in place, in spite of Bobby's turning away. "Robert, go get some ice. Don't worry, son, head wounds always bleed like crazy. He's all right—or will be once we get this stitched up."

Robert did as he was told, and DJ put her arms around Billy, who was crying just as hard. "Hey, you're not hurt."

Lindy carried the now hiccuping twin to the bleachers and sat with him on her lap. Blood stained her silk blouse and pants. She had a smear of blood across her cheek and more on her hands. When the ice came, she put the Ziploced bag against the wound and held it in place with her other hand.

DJ and Gran swapped grins. This was the woman who thought she couldn't be a mother?

"I knew she had it in her all along." Gran wrapped an arm around DJ's waist, patting the twins' legs in the same motion. Both twins had taken the same position, legs wrapped around the Randall who held them, cheeks into chests and arms around necks.

Later when DJ returned to the horse line, she thought about the look Robert had given Lindy and her charge as they'd gotten into his car to go to the emergency room. Gooey looks for sure.

The next night, after the entire show was finished and the horses were all back in their proper stalls, the family gathered at Gran and Joe's for dinner. Bobby proudly showed everyone his five black-thread stitches.

Billy moped around, his lower lip stuck out.

"Come here, B, I have a surprise for you." DJ took his hand and led him into Gran's studio. She set him up on the table and picked up a drawing pencil. With deft strokes, she drew lines in the same spot as Bobby's.

He giggled.

"Now, let's check that out." She carried him into the bathroom so he could see himself in the mirror.

"I gots stitches, too." He smacked a kiss on her cheek. She set him down, and he dashed off announcing the change as he ran.

The look Robert gave her made DJ feel warm inside. It had been such a little thing. But then, little things were important to kids. She ought to know.

She strolled back into the living room and looked over at her mother. Lindy was just reaching up to hand Robert something. The diamond ring twinkled on her left hand.

DJ crossed the room and leaned over the back of her mother's chair. "So, is there something you need to tell all of us?"

"I wanted to tell you first." Lindy looked up over her shoulder. "Is it okay?"

"Fine with me. But what about being scared?"

"I learned that thinking about something that's coming is always worse than the actual event. With God's grace and a lot of love, I think we'll make it."

"Me too." DJ took her mother's hand. "Oh, and I better get a plan started if we're going to have a wedding."

She looked up to catch the twinkle in her grandmother's eyes and the slight shake of the white-crowned head. *That's right, Gran, no more plans. At least not for other people. Let them make their own.* She made an *O* with her thumb and forefinger and showed it to Gran.

Gran smiled and nodded.

But, then again, maybe just a teeny *little plan.*

Out of the Blue

An unexpected phone call from the biological father DJ has never met leaves her flustered and plagued by questions. Why, after fourteen years of silence, is this stranger suddenly interested in getting to know her? Discover the answers in book #4 of the HIGH HURDLES series!